Andrew Dickson White, Oscar Browning

The Life of Bartolomeo Colleoni, of Anjou and Burgundy

Andrew Dickson White, Oscar Browning

The Life of Bartolomeo Colleoni, of Anjou and Burgundy

ISBN/EAN: 9783337196851

Printed in Europe, USA, Canada, Australia, Japan

Cover: Foto ©Raphael Reischuk / pixelio.de

More available books at **www.hansebooks.com**

THE LIFE

OF

BARTOLOMEO COLLEONI,

OF ANJOU AND BURGUNDY.

BY

OSCAR BROWNING.

PRINTED FOR THE ARUNDEL SOCIETY.

1891.

THE LIFE

OF

BARTOLOMEO COLLEONI.

THE LIFE

OF

BARTOLOMEO COLLEONI,

OF ANJOU AND BURGUNDY.

BY

OSCAR BROWNING.

PRINTED FOR THE ARUNDEL SOCIETY.

1891.

CHISWICK PRESS:—CHARLES WHITTINGHAM AND CO., TOOKS COURT,
CHANCERY LANE.

PREFACE.

THE materials I have used for the present life of Bartolomeo Colleoni have been in the main the following. I have taken as a foundation the work of Spino, " Historia della vita et fatti dell' eccelentissimo Capitano di guerra Bartolomeo Coglione scritta per M. Pietro Spino, In Vinetia appresso Gratioso Percaccino MDLXIX.," and the life of Colleoni in " Il Castello di Cavernago ei Conti Martinengo Colleoni, memorie storiche dell' avvocato Giuseppe Maria Bonomi, Bergamo, Fratelli Bolis 1884." Signor Bonomi has a large acquaintance with the archives of the Martinengo family, and has been instrumental in recovering the house of Colleoni in Bergamo for the municipality. The second edition of Spino, published at Bergamo, MDCCXXXII, contains two funeral orations and some additional information. The life of Spino is founded on that by Cornazzano, a poet who lived with Colleoni at Malpaga. The life, written in Latin, is contained in the Thesaurus of Graevius. I have not found it of any great value. I am also indebted to a life of Colleoni by Professor Gabriele Rosa, kindly lent me by the author. He is well acquainted with the history of the time of which he treats. The "Annali d' Italia," by Muratori, have been constantly in my hands, as also the "Histoire des Republiques Italiennes," by Sismondi. There is some difficulty in correlating the personal history of Colleoni with the history of his time, because his biographers and panegyrists attribute to him exploits which, in ordinary historians, are referred to other people. No one who attempts to write the life of Colleoni can dispense with the magnificently printed work, "Institutio Pii Loci Magnificae Pietatis Bergomi &c. Bergomi MDCLV.," which contains, also, Colleoni's will, with its codicils. I found in the library at Bergamo abstracts of papers in the Venetian archives relating to Colleoni; these I had copied, and I have used them in my book. I have paid several visits to Bergamo and its neighbourhood, and in the exploration of sites connected with Colleoni's life have been greatly assisted by Da Ponte's "Dizionario Odeporico" Bergamo, 1819, an admirable work of its kind.

The best authority for the visit of King Christian of Denmark to Italy I have found to be the "Holstein Chronicle," quoted by Hvitfeld in his History of Christian I., published in 1599. It has been translated for me from the black letter Danish by Mr. Bain of the British Museum, to whom the best thanks of the Arundel Society are due. I have been able to make some corrections from the German translation of the same chronicle in the British Museum. I am much obliged to Professor Henry Middleton and Mr.

Edmund Oldfield for having looked through the proof sheets, and also to Mr. Charles Sayle, of St. John's College, Cambridge, for assisting me in preparing the index.

It is possible that many interesting details of Colleoni's life have escaped my research. In this case I shall be obliged to anyone who will communicate them to me.

OSCAR BROWNING.

KING'S COLLEGE, CAMBRIDGE,
March 16th, 1891.

LIST OF ILLUSTRATIONS.

GENEALOGY OF THE COLLEONI FAMILY.

(FROM SPINO.)

GISALBERTO COLLIONI.

SOZZO. 1159, 1161.

ALBERTO. 1159, 1173.

GUGLIELMO, Console di Giustizia. 1152, 1161.

CARPIGLIONE. 1173, 1189.

ROGERIO, Console di Giustizia, 1230; Compilator de Statuti, 1237.

ALBERICO, Console di Giustizia, 1191.

GISALBERTO. 1254, 1255.

FILIPPO. 1254 1255.

GISALBERTO, Consigliere Nunzio; Difensore della Città, 1293; Conservator della Pace, 1309. 1359.

GALEAZZO. 1359.

CAPIGLIATA, Capitan Generale della S.R. Chiesa, 1370. 1359.

GUIDOTTO. 1406.

GUARDINO, Podestà di Ravenna, e Capitano d'Alessandria, 1392. 1406.

PAOLO DETTO PUHÒ. 1406.

PIERO. 1412.

DONDACCIO.

GIANGUARDINO.

GIOVANNI. 1406.

TESTINO.

GUARDINO.

PAOLO.

ANTONIO.

BARTOLOMEO, CAPITAN GENERALE.

CARPIGLIATA.

GIANPIETRO. 1475-

ISOTTA.

ORSINA.

CATERINA.

MEDEA.

The dates appended to the names refer to the years in which the persons to whom they belong were known to have been alive.

THE LIFE OF BARTOLOMEO COLLEONI.

AMONG the many monuments of mediæval Italy which cover the plains of Lombardy, none is more interesting than the castle of Trezzo, seated on the right bank of the Adda about midway on its passage from the gorges of the lower Alps to the broad waters of the Po. The green rushing river winds round a promontory which is almost an island. The massive castle rises in the midst. It is built of closely compacted blocks of pudding-stone mixed with courses of brick. In its present ruined condition it presents an untidy appearance to a close inspection, but in the days of its prime it was faced with smooth slabs of stone on which no foot or scaling-ladder could rest. Descending steeply into the river or rising from foundations of precipitous rock, it seemed to defy attack. It was connected with the left bank by a triple bridge of strong construction, the lower path leading to the dungeons, the middle way to the quarters of the garrison, while the upper road would conduct the master of the castle and his ladies to their chambers. The castle was built by Barnabò Visconti, and the bridge was destroyed by Carmagnola. From the tower of the keep the eye ranges over a view rich in beauty and in historical asso-

B

ciations. To the south the plain of Lombardy is lost in the
haze, watered by canals, teeming with maize and vine, dotted
with countless *campanili*. To the east, near at hand, is the
hill city of Bergamo, far away to the west is discerned
the slender spire which crowns the marble *duomo* of Milan.
To the north the eye, after plunging from the giddy height
into the lovely waters of the Adda, rises to the hills. The
Resegone of Lecco bounds the view; still nearer are the hills
which encircle the monastery of Pontida, the birthplace of the
Lombard league. Conspicuous at the edge of the plain is a
conical hill topped by a ruin called the Torre dei Colleoni, the
birthplace of that noble family, and just below is the church-
tower of Solza, a little village on the Adda about six miles
from Trezzo, where Bartolomeo was born in the year 1400.
The room in which he saw the light is still reverenced by his
fellow-countrymen.

The Colleoni were an ancient family of Bergamo. The
city was torn asunder, like other Italian towns, by the rival
factions of Guelf and Ghibelline. The Ghibelline cause was
sustained by the Suardi, the Guelf by the Rivola and the
Colleoni. A document dated Bergamo, 1101, bears the signa-
ture of Olricus Sivardus, and Gisilbertus Co-léone, the lion's
head, which testifies to the ancient spelling of the name. In
1182 and 1189 we find a Carpiglione Coglione holding an
honourable position at Isola and at Calusco. The son of
Carpiglione was Alberigo, of Alberigo Ghisalberto, who was a
judge, of Ghisalberto Galeazzo, of Galeazzo Carpigliata, who
was a powerful captain under Pope Urban V. (1362-1370).
Carpigliata had two sons, Guardino and Guidotto; Guidotto

had a son, Paulo, familiarly corrupted into Puhò, who was the father of Bartolomeo. We read of a Sozzan dei Coglioni who was appointed a judge of appeal in Bergamo with remainder to his descendants by the Emperor Frederick II. in the year 1224, also of a Tresado Coglioni, who became Podestà of Lodi in 1270. In 1373, Barnabò Visconti, in order to avenge the death of his son Ambrogio, attacked Guglielmo Colleoni, and drove him into the monastery of Pontida, and put him to death after he had surrendered upon promise of having his life spared.

The name of Bartolomeo's mother was Ricardona Valvasori dei Saiguini. His father was not very wealthy, but he possessed the two castles of Solza and Chignolo. On September 3rd, 1402, when Colleoni was two years old, Gian Galeazzo Visconti, ruler of Milan, died at Marignano on the Lambro; he divided his dominions between his two legitimate sons Gian Maria and Filippo Maria, and an illegitimate son Gabriello whom he had recognized. As his children were under age he confided the regency to his wife Caterina, with the assistance of a council which consisted of Francesco Gonzaga, lord of Mantua, Count Antonio of Urbino, Jacopo del Verme, Pandolfo Malateste, Count Alberico da Barbiano, and Francesco Barbavara of Novara. The regents soon began to quarrel amongst themselves and to rebel against the Duchess, being disgusted at the favour which she exhibited towards Barbavara. The large territory so laboriously amassed was violently torn asunder. Ugo Cavalcabò seized upon Cremona and Crema, Franchino Rusca made himself master of Como, the Guelf party occupied a large part of

Brescia, Bergamo was torn asunder by conflicting factions. In the general confusion Puhò Colleoni seized upon the castle of Trezzo, a most important bulwark of the Milanese territory towards the territory of Bergamo. It is said that Puhò, having established himself at Trezzo, incited his first cousins Giovanni, Dondaccio, Testino and Paolo to share his fortunes, as they were exiled from Bergamo and were in a poor condition. One day the four brothers, led by Giovanni the eldest, attacked Puhò as he was playing at draughts, killed him, and threw his widow into one of the dungeons of the fortress. Bartolomeo took refuge with a schoolmaster in the mountains of Bergamo, until, after the lapse of a year, he rejoined his mother at Solza. Even here he was not left in peace, but was thrown into prison by Giorgio Benzone, lord of Crema, until he could pay from his mother's dowry some debts which were due from his elder brother Antonio to that tyrant.

On May 16th, 1412, Gian Maria Visconti, who was detested for his cruelty, was murdered by a body of conspirators while he was hearing mass in the church of S. Gottardo. His brother Filippo Maria now became Duke of Milan, and his first object was to recover the dominions of his father. The castle of Trezzo was taken by the *condottiere* Carmagnola in 1416, and the Colleoni were turned out. Probably before this time Bartolomeo had entered the service of Filippo Arcelli, lord of Piacenza, where he received the ordinary education of a page. In course of time Arcelli was himself defeated by Filippo Maria Visconti, and the bodies of his son and brothers were impaled upon the walls before his eyes. Colleoni had to fly for his life. He betook himself to the south of Italy, where the principal *condottiere* captains of the age were then engaged. At this time the kingdom of Naples was in a state of the utmost confusion. The titular Queen was Joanna II., the degenerate descendant of the great Charles of Anjou. Pope Martin V. who had first crowned and then found that he could not tolerate her, had called in as a rival Louis III. of Anjou, a scion of the house of Valois. Joanna in 1421 proclaimed Alfonso of Aragon her successor, whom thirteen years later she deserted for René of Anjou, titular Duke of Lorraine. After a series of long and ruinous wars, peace was eventually secured by the entrance of Alfonso into Naples in 1422. The grand constable of the Queen was Sforza Attendolo, who from being a simple wood-cutter had risen to the position of the most powerful *condottiere* of his age. The Pope now sent for Sforza and persuaded him to support the cause of the Duke of Anjou. He marched to Naples, returned to Queen Joanna his insignia as constable, and ordered her to renounce the crown. Besides the proclamation of Alfonso she thought it advisable to call in the assistance of Braccio, count of Montone, whom she invested with the principality of Capua. His reputation as a mercenary general was only second to that of Sforza. Braccio took possession of Sulmona and marched to the capture of Aversa, where Sforza met him. At this time Jacopo Caldora, one of the barons who had revolted against Queen Joanna and had joined Sforza, suddenly came over to the side of Braccio. The two generals marched together to Naples, and . arrived there on June 26th, 1421, just at the moment when

King Alfonso entered the harbour with his fleet. Not long after this Queen Joanna quarrelled with Alfonso and called Sforza to her aid.

Into the surging sea of discord the young Bartolomeo was thrown. He first attached himself to Braccio, who knowing nothing of him except his appearance, placed him amongst his *ragazzi*, who were little better than stable-boys. So he left Braccio and joined Caldora, who was then fighting on the side of Sforza. A story that he crossed the sea to take service in France, was captured by pirates near Marseilles, and was brought back to Naples, has probably but little foundation. Caldora first gave him command of twenty horses and then of fifteen more. It is said that he attracted the attention, and possibly the love, of Queen Joanna, who gave him the well-known badge, which he constantly used, of two lions' heads joined by a red band, between two narrower bands of white.

Towards the close of 1423, Braccio undertook the siege of the city of Aquila, which had declared for Queen Joanna against the King of Aragon. The siege lasted for more than a year. It was during its progress that Sforza, hastening to the relief of the city, was drowned at the mouth of the river Pescara on January 4th, 1424. The stream was swollen by the tide, Sforza was impatient to reach the opposite bank. When in the midst of the stream he turned round to catch a drowning page by the hair. His horse lost its footing, and he fell from the saddle. Twice he raised mailed hands in supplication, but his helmet and his armour weighed him down, and his body was never recovered.

Braccio had a presentiment that he should not long survive his rival. He was defeated by Caldora on June 2nd, 1424, outside the walls of Aquila. He was wounded, but not mortally, refused to have his hurt attended to or to take any food, and died in a few days. The principality which he had founded was broken up. In these operations Colleoni obtained great distinction. During the next four years Colleoni remained in the service of Caldora. This general sent his son Giovanni Antonio into the Marches to secure some of the possessions of Braccio. As he was too young to be entrusted with the entire command of the army, Colleoni was appointed to look after him. He apparently did everything that was expected of him, and returned with distinction to Naples. In August, 1428, the people of Bologna rose against the Pope, burned the palace of the cardinal-legate, and established a republic. Pope Martin begged from Queen Joanna the assistance of Caldora, who at the close of the year marched against the city. Bologna was not reduced to obedience till the end of August, 1429.

After this Colleoni left Caldora, and took service under Carmagnola, who was commander-in-chief of the armies of Venice. On October 15th, 1431, Carmagnola was besieging Cremona, and seeing that the garrison were keeping very careless watch, sent a detachment to seize the fortress of San Luca, to the north of the town. They captured it, and held it for two days, but not being supported by the general, were obliged to retire. This was the principal cause of the misunderstanding which now arose between Carmagnola and the Republic, which eventually led to his execution. Pietro

Spino tells us in his biography of Colleoni, that the leaders
of the attack were Colleoni, Mocenigo da Lugo, and the
son of Ugolino Cavalcabò, lord of Cremona, and that Colleoni
was the first to mount the battlements.   Cavalcabò expected
to obtain the assistance of his countrymen within the walls.
Whatever may have been the true circumstances of the case,
Carmagnola was suddenly summoned to Venice on April 8th,
1432, was brought to trial before the Council of Ten, and on
May 5th in the same year was beheaded, with a gag between
his teeth, between the two columns on the Piazetta of St.
Mark.

Colleoni now took service under the great Republic.
Carmagnola had entrusted him with forty horsemen, he now
had command of eighty.   It must be remembered that in
the mercenary companies each lance or *cavallo* comprised
three men, the *caporale* or man-at-arms, the *piatta* or squire,
and the *ragazzo* or page.   The first two rode chargers, and
the page had a pony as a nag.   Five lances usually made
up a *posta*, and five *poste* made a *bandiera*.   There was also
generally an officer for every ten lances.   Peace had been
made between Milan and Venice by the treaty of Ferrara,
signed on April 19th, 1428.   The Venetian dominion was
extended as far as the Adda, including the great cities of
Brescia and Bergamo.   The truce did not last long.   Francesco Sforza, who had entered into the service of the Visconti,
urged a renewal of the struggle, in which Carmagnola played
a prominent part on the side of Venice.   After his execution,
the Venetian army crossed the Oglio, and took the castles of
Bordelano, Romanengo, Fontanella, and Soncino.   They over-

ran the Val Camonica and the Valtellina. Piccinino, the general of the Visconti, was at first beaten, but won afterwards victories at Lecco. Colleoni is said to have been equally conspicuous in victory and in defeat. Together with the famous *condottiere*, Stefano da Narni, called Gattamelata, he collected the fugitives, and brought them through the mountain paths of the Val Sassina and the Val San Martino. The Venetians now intrusted the command of their armies to Gian Francesco Gonzaga, Marquis of Mantua, who recovered the Val Camonica and the Valtellina.

A second peace of Ferrara was concluded in April, 1433, On February 2nd, 1435, Joanna II. of Naples died. Her will appointed as her heir René, Count of Provence and Duke of Anjou, the father of the unfortunate Margaret, wife of Henry VI. of England. The validity of this testament was contested by Alfonso, who hurried from Sicily to defend his kingdom, while the Pope declared that in the failure of the heirs of Charles of Anjou, the crown of Naples reverted to him as a Papal fief. The Duke of Milan took the side of René against Alfonso, and sent a Genoese fleet to the rescue of Gaeta. The fleet of Alfonso was defeated in August, 1435, off the island of Ponza, and Alfonso, with his brother John, King of Navarre, was taken prisoner. They were conducted first to Genoa and then to Milan, where Alfonso by his ability and charm completely subdued the capricious Filippo Maria. He persuaded him that it was his real interest to prefer the advancement of Aragon to that of France, and left him a devoted friend. This sudden and romantic change produced a great impression in Europe.

The Pope was in despair. Soon after this the Florentine
exiles persuaded Filippo Maria to attack their city, and a league
was formed between Florence and Venice, so that the great
war began again in the spring of 1437. Gonzaga was ordered
to cross the Adda, which he attempted to do by a bridge of
fishing-boats; he was, however, compelled by Piccinino to retreat, and retired to Bolgare.

Spino relates a great service which Colleoni rendered to
the Venetians at this time. While the Venetian army was
posted at Bolgare, on the Cherio, Piccinino, in considerably
greater strength, was encamped near Malpaga, about two
miles distant. Piccinino proceeded to occupy Monticelli in the
rear of the Venetians, and a retreat became necessary for them.
Gonzaga advised the abandonment of all their baggage and
encampments, and a hasty night march to Palazzuolo, where
they would be able to cross the Oglio. Colleoni opposed the
cowardly conduct of deserting their standards, and argued
eloquently for an immediate advance to Pontoglio, which was
easier and shorter. Piccinino, reinforced by Ludovico Gonzaga, who deserted the Venetians and his father, attacked
them in the rear, but the Venetian army got away safely. The
field in which this great danger assailed them has ever since
been known as the " Field of Fear." By these movements
Bergamo was left deserted, but Colleoni and Diotesalvi Lupo
hastened to its defence. Piccinino, instead of attacking it,
marched to the castle of Calepio on the Oglio which was defended by Count Trusardo. After holding out twenty days,
it surrendered on May 25th, 1437, and was destroyed by
Piccinino. That general then laid waste the territory of the

Bergamasque, but, being successfully resisted in the mountains by Bartolomeo Colleoni, turned his attention to Brescia. The Venetian army had, however, suffered such considerable losses, that the Senate transferred the command from Gonzaga to Gattamelata. Colleoni, seeing that Bergamo was safe, recovered the castle of Gorzone, in the Val Camonica, from the enemy, and hastened to the post of danger at Brescia. Here he received an embassy from the Venetians. A hundred lances were added to his command, and he was placed in entire control of the infantry.

In the year 1439 Gattamelata was besieged in Brescia. If the garrison was to hold out it was absolutely necessary to diminish the number of mouths which had to be fed. The plain was held by the enemy's troops, and the only escape was through the mountains. Leaving a force of six hundred horse and a thousand foot behind them, Gattamelata and Colleoni passed by Santo Eusebio, the lake of Idro, and the Val di Ledro into the valley of the Adige. They were met on the banks of the Sarca by the troops of Piccinino under the command of Ludovico dal Verme, but they succeeded in driving them back, and on the fourth day from leaving Brescia, reached the territory of Verona in safety. Passing into the Val Lagarnia they took the towns of Borgo, Corvaria, and Penetre, and especially the town of Torbole, situated on the extremity of the lake which was specially convenient for the convoy of provisions to Brescia. That town now began seriously to feel the pangs of hunger. Soldo, the historian, relates that he saw a hundred children in the market-place crying, " Bread, bread for the love of God!" The population fed on dogs, horses, and even weeds. At the end of the siege the thirty thousand inhabitants were reduced to fifteen thousand, and wolves came down into the city itself to seek their prey. Piccinino was in possession of Peschiera and the southern shores of Garda. The Venetians came to the conclusion that the only means of forcing a passage was to convey a flotilla on to the lake of Garda. In the space of fifteen days, with the help of two thousand oxen and an expense of fifteen thousand sequins, they placed upon the lake twenty-five boats and six galleys. The ships were rowed and towed up the Adige and dragged by main force over the mountain which separates the valley of that river from the lake at Torbole. Spino gives the credit of this bold project to Colleoni, but the Venetian historians assign it to Niccolò Sorbolo, a native of Candia, who was certainly the principal engineer in the operation. Shortly after this Colleoni's command was increased to three hundred lances, and he was intrusted with the government and the defence of the city of Verona. Francesco Sforza now joined the Venetian army in the hope of one day succeeding to the inheritance of the Visconti. He united his troops with those of Gattamelata at the head of the lake of Garda. Piccinino was encamped not far off. The allies attacked him at the castle of Tenna, completely defeated him and took Gonzaga, Cesare Martinengo and Sacramoro Visconti prisoners. Piccinino escaped, carried off in a sack, like a dead body, by a sturdy German. He reappeared at Verona, which he succeeded in wresting from the Venetians, all but the quarters of Castel Vecchio and San Felice. Three days later Sforza and Colleoni succeeded in recovering it. Gattamelata became seriously ill, and was obliged to retire to Padua, where he died three years later. In the following year, 1440, Piccinino was sent by the Duke of Milan into the Marches and Tuscany. While there he heard of the victory which the Venetian flotilla on the lake of Garda had gained over that of the Duke of Milan. This led to the raising of the siege of Brescia, which Sforza and Colleoni entered in triumph in June, 1440.

Colleoni continued to fight under the orders of Sforza against Piccinino, and a number of his most illustrious exploits were attributed to his chief. In the battle of Cignano, which lasted from morning to evening, Sforza would undoubtedly have been defeated if it had not been for the assistance of Colleoni who was summoned from Brescia. Shortly after this when Piccinino crossed the Oglio at Ponte Vico into the territory of Cremona, Colleoni occupied the passage of Pontoglio, and was thus able to defend the whole of the Bergamasque. Another conflict took place between Romano and Martinengo of which Sforza gave the full credit to Colleoni. The peace of Capriana was at last made at the close of July, 1441. It was confirmed by the marriage of Sforza to Bianca Maria the daughter of Filippo Visconti, then sixteen years old. Bianca brought with her the city of Cremona as a dowry, and the beautiful church of San Sigismundo, about two miles outside the walls, was erected in 1463 to commemorate the event. The altar-piece of the high altar painted by Giulio Campi represents Francesco Sforza and his wife being presented to the Virgin by San Grisante and St. Jerome.

In recognition of these services the Council of Ten at Venice passed a decree on April 3rd, 1441, declaring Colleoni to be one of the principal *condottieri* of the republic and necessary to their security. They confirmed him in his emoluments and invested him with the fiefs of Romano, Covo and Antegnate. Romano is a large town south of Bergamo formed out of a Roman prætorian camp. The castle was frequently inhabited by Colleoni, and a large number of houses still standing, decorated with the lion of Saint Mark, were left by Colleoni to the municipality in his will. Covo and Antegnate are villages in the neighbourhood of Romano both provided with castles. Colleoni was to have all the possessions of Counts Pietro and Giovanni di Covo, who had rebelled against the state, but on the condition that these lands must first come into the possession of the Republic. This condition was fulfilled by the conclusion of the peace of which we have already spoken, and the investiture was confirmed by a ducal patent on March 4th, 1443. This later date corresponds with Colleoni's visit to Milan, and the step was probably taken with the design of retaining him in the service of the Republic. Piccinino, discontented with the peace which deprived him of his employment, took service with the Pope, and induced his Holiness to deprive Sforza of his position as standard-bearer of the Church. According to the historian Sanuto, a new league was formed on October 16th, 1442, between King Alfonso, Piccinino, and the Duke of Milan against the Venetians, the Florentines and Francesco Sforza. Colleoni marched with a body of fifteen hundred lances to fight against Piccinino. At this time Gherardo

Dandolo was *provedditore* of Venice, an excellent man but rough-mannered. It was his duty to reduce the armies of the Republic to a peace footing, and consequently to deprive Colleoni of some of his soldiers. Colleoni complaining of this, and demanding thirty-four thousand ducats which were due to him as arrears of pay, was met by haughty and contemptuous language. Consequently he left the service of the Republic to their great dismay and joined Filippo Maria Visconti, the command of the militia held by him being given to Diotesalvi Lupo, who was the first to arm infantry with guns and pistols.

Colleoni visited Milan at the beginning of 1443 and was received with great honour by the Duke. He was entertained with all his family at the public expense. The duke frequently invited him to dinner, and held long private conversations with him. He also invested him with the castle of Adorno in the territory of Pavia, which was to serve as a residence for his wife Madonna Tisbe, to whom he also made a present of valuable jewels. The consequence of this was that Colleoni deserted the service of Venice for that of the Duke. Sanuto writes in his diary on the date September. 28th, 1443, "News arrived of the flight of Bartolommeo "Colleoni from our signory and his passage to the Duke "of Milan. To begin with he had no more than three lances, "and the signory gave him two hundred lances and a hundred "and fifty hired infantry. He is also our subject." This "treason" as it was called produced a great effect on the mind of the Venetians.

The first expedition of Colleoni under his new master

was to Sinigaglia to take a position between the two armies of Piccinino and Sforza. His instructions were to stay there till he was attacked, and to prevent too serious a conflict taking place between them. He was successful in this difficult task, but after his recall Sforza defeated Nicolo Piccinino at Monte Lamo, and afterwards his son Francesco with great slaughter at Mont' Olmo. Piccinino was so overcome with grief that he died at Milan in the middle of October, 1444.

In the following year Colleoni was sent to repress some disturbances in the territory of Bologna, and in 1446 to recover Cremona for the Duke. This city had been given to Francesco Sforza as a dowry with his wife Bianca. The Duke, however, declared that it had only been intrusted to him for money which had not been paid and should therefore revert to his possession. Whilst Colleoni was engaged in this operation he was suddenly seized and thrown into prison at Monza, where he remained for more than a year, till the death of the Duke on August 13th, 1447. This extraordinary step gave rise to many rumours. Some believed that in the previous year, when Colleoni was opposed to the Venetians, he had shown a disposition to enter into negotiations with them. Others thought that his imprisonment was due to the jealousy of Francesco Piccinino. Another report was that Colleoni was taking steps to become the head of the Guelf party, another that the captured cities paid more honour to Colleoni than they did to Filippo, while some attributed it to the ancient jealousy of the Colleoni family by the treasonable capture of Trezzo by Puhò. We need not, at this date, look

MAX · + BARTOLOMEVS COLEON · ANDEGAVEN · ET · BVRGVND · BELLI · DVX

PROPRIA GENTIS ET
MILITIAE. INSIGNIA.

for any other reason than the wilfulness and treachery of the
Duke himself. Colleoni was ordered into the territory of
Piacenza. As he was crossing the Po he was seized by Nicolo
Guerriero and taken into the castle of Piacenza. In the meantime everything which Colleoni possessed at Adorno had been
removed to Pavia, but was honestly returned to him when he
was set at liberty. Spino enables us to quote an interesting
letter of the Duke's to Colleoni's tenants at Romano.

"To our beloved commune and men of Romano the
"Duke of Milan, Count of Pavia and Anghiari, Lord of
"Genoa.

"Our beloved, that you may not be astonished, and be
"distressed at anything which has been done against the
"person of the honourable Bartolomeo Colleoni, we advise
"you that what has been done, has not been done because we
"have any intention of doing him harm, nor of inflicting any
"injury on his person. Any one who behaves ill to him, will
"behave ill to us. But it has been done that we may be
"more clear from any trouble. We advise you and comfort
"you that you may be of good will and cheerful, because
"in a short time he will be in favour, and that in a way to
"be greater than ever, and you shall be consoled and well
"content. We comfort you therefore and charge you to
"have good care of the land, and to keep it and guard it in
"the name of the said Colleoni. And if you have need of
"any assistance in defence for it, ask for it, because we will
"do for the defence of that land, what we have previously
"done before the new line of conduct taken by us towards the
"said Bartolomeo, and even better still, and as we act towards

" our lands which are most in favour with us. Given at
" Milan, Sept. 26, 1446."

Whilst Colleoni was in prison the fortunes of the Duke
went on from bad to worse. The Venetians occupied in turn
Ghiara d'Adda, Crema, and Lodi. They passed the Adda at
Casciano, and devastated the territory of Pavia, threatening
even Milan itself. They then conquered the fortress of
Brivio in the Brianza, together with Cassano and Lecco. In
this distress Filippo did everything to gain Sforza over to
his side. Sforza asked the counsel of Cosimo de' Medici as to
what course he should pursue. Florence was beginning to be
jealous of the success of the Venetians, so that Cosimo
advised Sforza to think of his own interests, and if he had no
money to give Pisa to his soldiers. Just at this moment
Filippo Maria Visconti died, on August 13th, 1447, in his
palace at the Porta Zobbia. He left no male heir. Immediately after his death there were cries of " Long live
liberty !" The people of Milan established the Ambrosian
Republic. Other cities followed the example. Parma proclaimed a republic ; Lodi and Piacenza asserted their in-
dependence, and joined themselves to Venice. Pavia, where
Madonna Tisbe and her daughter were living, surrendered
to Sforza. The news of these events was not long in
reaching Monza. Colleoni, learning or suspecting what had
happened, determined to escape. He pretended to be
seriously ill, and asked for bands of linen to wrap round
his body. He fastened one end of these to a bench and
let himself down into the ditch. The escape was discovered.
The tocsin rang ; all the neighbourhood was in arms. In

the confusion Colleoni crawled unperceived from the ditch, and joined those who were calling out his name. In the crowd he met an old soldier of his, Giorgetto Poma of Bergamo, who furnished him with a horse, upon which he fled to Landriano, where he was received with enthusiasm by his own troops. He then betook himself to Pavia, where he rejoined his wife. Sforza refused to give up Pavia to Milan, but nevertheless the city took him into her service in order to continue the war against Venice. On his side fought Colleoni, Francesco and Jacopo Piccinino, and also Carlo Gonzaga, the Marquis of Mantua, who had deserted the Republic. The first step of Sforza in his new command was to assault Piacenza and take it by storm. It was then given up to plunder and every kind of horror for fifty days.

Charles Duke of Orleans, son of Valentino Visconti, and titular lord of Asti, managed to rescue that city after the death of Filippo. The king of France sent him an army of about three thousand cavalry and infantry, under the command of Rinaldo de Dudresnay. With this assistance he attacked the territory of Alessandria, captured a number of castles, giving no quarter to the enemy. In the beginning of October Colleoni was sent against him with a thousand horse, and Astore da Faenza with five hundred. Colleoni engaged with them in the territory of Bosco, entirely defeated them, and took Dudresnay prisoner, whom he confined in his castle of Romano. After this exploit he attacked the territory of Tortona, and reduced it to submission. He was next sent to attack Lecco, which was in the hands of the Venetians. The bridge across the Adda had two strong towers at each end and

one in the centre, all strongly garrisoned. Colleoni had taken
two of these towers, and was preparing to attack the third,
when the place was relieved by Micheletto Attendolo, who had
marched to its assistance through the valley of San Martino.

For some reasons which are imperfectly known to us, Colleoni
now determined to desert Sforza and to return to the allegiance
of Venice. This happened when the Milanese armies were
besieging Lodi, on June 15th, 1448. He took with him a force
of about fifteen hundred men. The Venetian army was now
encamped in the plain of Bergamo, under the command of
Michele Attendolo. Colleoni received a salary of ten thousand
ducats, and was confirmed in the possession of Romano, Covo,
and Antegnate. Many skirmishes took place in the neighbourhood of Caravaggio, which the Venetians were especially
anxious to preserve. The decisive battle was fought on September 15th. The Venetians began the attack when Sforza was
either at mass or at breakfast, suspecting nothing. The soldiers
immediately around him were routed, but fortune soon changed.
He sent two thousand cavalry through a wood to attack the
Venetians in the rear. Their defeat was immediate and com-
plete; of twelve thousand Venetian cavalry only fifteen hundred escaped. The terror of the calamity deprived Brescia
and Bergamo of all power of resistance. Sforza entered Caravaggio, and crossing the Oglio found himself master of both
these provinces. The battle of Caravaggio claimed many
victims. None was more lamented by Colleoni than Antoni-
azzo, who had grown up with him from a little boy, and who
now had command of a hundred lances. He sent his body
to be buried with all honour in the city of Romano. After

the battle of Caravaggio the government of Milan ordered Sforza to divide his forces, and to attack Bergamo and Lodi at the same time. He prepared to turn his arms against Brescia, hoping that it might remain to him as the prize of victory. Hoping also to come to terms with the Venetians, he set at liberty all the prisoners which had been taken at the battle of Caravaggio. In fact, on October 18th, 1448, thirty-three days after the battle, he made a treaty with the Republic of St. Mark on the condition that he should evacuate all the territories which he had conquered in the provinces of Bergamo and Brescia; that he should give up the rights of the Visconti and the Milanese over the territory of Crema and the Ghiara d'Adda, and should cede them to the Venetians. The Venetians on their side engaged to assist Sforza in conquering the dominions of the Visconti. They promised him four thousand horse and two thousand infantry, and to pay thirteen thousand florins a month until Milan was reduced. When he was master of Milan, Venice and that duchy were to be on terms of alliance. Colleoni commanded the cavalry which the Venetians sent to the assistance of Sforza. It was first employed in recovering the castles in the provinces of Bergamo and Brescia, among which were Martinengo and Romano. Colleoni was then sent to reduce Parma on the other side of the Apennines. The city was torn asunder by discordant factions, and after having in vain waited for assistance from Venice, submitted to Colleoni. That general then returned to Lombardy to assist Sforza in reducing the Milanese.

At this time Mary of Savoy, the widow of Filippo Maria

Visconti, who resided at Milan, where she was respected by the magistrates and the people, negotiated an alliance between her brother Louis Duke of Savoy and the republic of Milan. The King of France, Charles VII., gave to the duke the services of Jean des Compeys, lord of Torrens. He had an army of six thousand horsemen, two-thirds of them Savoyards, so noted for their cruelty that the Italians called them barbarians. They invaded the territory of Novara, and Colleoni was sent against them. Colleoni was not allowed to cross the river Sesia, which formed the frontier between Milan and Piedmont. After a number of skirmishes, the first serious engagement took place on April 1st, 1449, in which Compeys and four hundred soldiers were taken prisoners. Three weeks later, on April 23rd, a still more serious battle was fought on the flat ground between Borgomanero and Carpignano. The fight was hotly contested. The Italians had their first experience of the archers of Picardy, who dismounted from horseback, tied their animals to trees, fixed pointed stakes in the ground so as to form a stockade, and fought behind its protection. At length the French, worn out by fatigue and by the weight of their arms, took refuge in flight; they were pursued for two miles and cut to pieces. A thousand prisoners were taken, amongst whom were Jacopo Celendo, Jacopo Aborte, and Gaspare Varesino. Whilst Colleoni was engaged in these exploits, Sforza was occupied in the siege of Vigevano, which submitted to him after a long resistance. The castle of that town, although built in the previous century, still bears the inscription " Ludovico Sforza Visconti," as he enlarged it and surrounded it with new galleries. He now recalled Colleoni from Novara, who returned to him with triumphal pomp, and was received with every mark of honour and distinction. Sforza pronounced his praises in a public assembly, and Colleoni was able to obtain for the people of Vigevano more favourable terms than had been accorded to Piacenza and other similar conquests. The fame of these victories of Colleoni over the French passed over the Alps and reached the ears of Charles the Bold and Louis XI., king of France.

After the submission of Vigevano Sforza proceeded, as he said, to "cut the green corn in all the territory of the Milanese." That city charged Enrico Panigarda to plead their cause with Venice. The Venetians began to perceive the error they had committed, and opened negotiations with Milan without Sforza's knowledge. Their operations were hastened by Sforza's treachery, who contrived that the towns of Crema and Lodi should be given up to him on September 11th. The Council of Ten now informed him that an armistice had been signed between Venice and the Ambrosian Republic and Colleoni was summarily recalled.

The peace between the two republics was signed at Brescia on September 27th, 1449, and communicated to Sforza three days later. By its conditions he was left with considerable power. He was to restore Lodi and surrender his claim on Milan and Como, but he was recognized as lord of Novara, Tortona, Alessandria, Pavia, Piacenza, Parma, and Cremona. He was, however, dissatisfied with these terms, and only concluded a delusive truce of twenty days whilst he allowed the negotiations for peace to drag on. At the expiration of the armistice he refused to ratify the treaty, upon which the Venetians determined to give active assistance to Milan. The commander-in-chief of their armies was Sigismundo Malatesta, and the most distinguished of his lieutenants was Bartolomeo Colleoni. They threw two bridges across the Adda, one of wood at Brivio, high up in the mountains, and one of boats at Trezzo, lower down the stream. They then marched towards Milan, but they found the plain so completely occupied by the troops of Sforza that they could make no progress. Colleoni, who seems to have possessed a kindred genius to Garibaldi in mountain warfare, determined to reach Milan by another route. He ascended the Val San Martino, crossed over a pass into the Val Sassina, then in possession of the Venetians, which runs from Lecco parallel to the lake of Como, and descended it to Bellano, which he took from Sforza, as well as Asso in the Brianza. Spino tells us that Colleoni now succeeded in effecting a junction with Jacopo Piccinino, and in relieving Milan, but the best authorities deny this, and say that all attempts to assist the beleaguered city were in vain. The town was experiencing all the horrors of famine. The rich were compelled to feed on horses, mules and dogs, while the poor were sustained by the roots and herbs which grew upon the ramparts. Thousands lay dead in the streets; thousands more took refuge in the country but were driven back by Sforza into the town. The government of Milan in despair met in the church of Santa Maria della Scala, and prepared to surrender their city into the hands of the Venetians. Whilst they were deliberating, the starving populace rose

in tumult on February 25th. The palace was attacked, one wing of which was occupied by the government, and the other by Maria Visconti, the widow of the last duke. Leonardo Venieri, the Venetian ambassador, while attempting to defend the palace, was cut down by the insurgents. This ended in offers of the sovereignty of Milan to Francesco Sforza, who made his triumphal entry into the town on March 25th, 1450. The Ambrosian Republic had lasted two years, seven months, and thirteen days.

Colleoni was now recalled, and was sent to Isola della Scala in the territory of Verona, on the borders of Mantua. He occupied himself in erecting a strong fortress on the Mantuan marshes. The command of the Venetian army was now divided between Sigismundo Malatesta, Gentile della Lionessa, the brother of Gattamelata, and Jacopo Piccinino. Colleoni was offended at being passed over, and began to think of deserting the service of the Venetians. They made various efforts to retain him. They sent envoys to him, on April 3rd, 1452, begging him to remain. They repeated the attempt ten days later, and asked the Pope and the King of Aragon to act as mediators. We are told by Spino that the government of Venice ordered his arrest while he was encamped at Montechiaro, and that he was in danger of suffering the fate of Carmagnola. Hearing the tramp of armed men, he leaped upon a horse, and rode at full gallop towards Mantua with only three followers. He was pursued by light cavalry soldiers, and his horse became weary. So he exchanged it for a mule belonging to a peasant, which he rode without a saddle, and arrived in safety at Mantua, where

E

he was received by the Duke Ludovico Gonzaga with distinguished honours. Colleoni's troops, amounting to more
than fifteen hundred *cavalli*, were captured in their quarters.
His wife and daughters were made prisoners, but a sum was
assigned for their support. Sanuto tells us that the money
which came into the hands of the Venetians belonging to
Colleoni amounted to between eighty and a hundred thousand
golden florins. Out of this a sum of two thousand ducats was
paid to Gherardo di Martinengo who had married Colleoni's
daughter Orsina. His fief of Romano was made over by the
Republic to Fermo Maffei. It may easily be supposed that
Ludovico Sforza did not neglect an opportunity of securing so
important an ally as Colleoni. He gave him a command of
two thousand horse, and five hundred infantry. He assigned
to him a larger stipend than he had asked for, and presented
him with a rich standard embroidered with the arms of Sforza,
a silver eagle on a shield of gold. The treaty between them
provided that in the war against Venice if Bergamo and
Brescia should be conquered Colleoni was to have on appro-
priate estate in one of these territories, and that the first
prisoners made by the Milanese should be given in exchange
for Madonna Tisbe and her daughters.

The war was renewed on May 16th, 1452. Cosimo dei
Medici and the French took the side of Sforza; Alfonso of
Naples and the Duke of Montferrat the side of the Venetians.
Sforza assembled his troops to the north of Cremona, and
crossing the Oglio at Pontevico invaded the territory of
Brescia. The strong castle of Pontevico held out for two
days, and the skill of Colleoni was conspicuous in its capture.

The Venetians formed their army in two divisions, crossed the Adda at Rivalta with one, and the Oglio at Pontoglio with the other. They penetrated as far as the suburbs of Milan, which they found well defended; they then retired into the district of Ghiara d'Adda, took the castle of Soncino, and secured the submission of all fortresses between Pontevico and Cremona, which they prepared to attack. Sforza did nothing to defend his favourite city, but remained in the territory of Brescia, the two armies being encamped opposite each other on either side of the Oglio. Porcelli, a contemporary Neapolitan poet, has left us an account of this campaign, which has been published by Muratori. He visited both armies, and flattered the generals on either side with indiscriminate adulation. Sforza had eighteen thousand horse, and three thousand infantry; the Venetians fifteen thousand horse, and six thousand foot soldiers. The people of Brescia appear to have kept up their spirits. On the day of the Assumption, August 15th, a comic tournament was held of horses and donkeys, while the women of loose character held a public wrestling match. The stress of the war was naturally turned against Colleoni's personal possessions. A tract of country close to his castle of Covo, which he had converted from a barren plain into flourishing corn-fields, was entirely laid waste. Out of ten of Colleoni's labourers who had gone out to cut straw, seven were thrown into the canal, and one had his eye cut out and his hand cut off, and was sent in that condition to report the news of what had occurred. For this Colleoni exacted a terrible vengeance. He made an attack upon Brescia, taking more than four hundred prisoners, and two thousand head of cattle. The Venetians were forced to raise the siege of Cremona, and to retire upon Brescia.

The Venetian army was encamped near Porzano, in a place so surrounded by marshes, that it was impossible to escape except by a very narrow passage. Sforza was posted about four miles off in a favourable position. He was anxious to bring about a decisive engagement. The Venetian commanders, Gentile of Lionessa, and Jacopo Piccinino, declined the challenge. Upon this Colleoni determined to lead an assault, which was entirely successful. The narrow pass which formed the only exit was bombarded by two large cannon, which took the Venetian columns in flank. Colleoni took the principal share in these operations. The war now passed into the territory of Lodi; the Venetians crossed the Adda by a bridge of boats at the monastery of Cereto. Sforza did his utmost to destroy it by throwing logs of wood into the upper river, and letting them be carried down by the rushing current; the Venetians opened the bridge in the centre and let the logs pass through. Several other assaults were made, both on the bridge and the outworks which defended it, but without success, until Sforza was obliged to invoke the aid of Colleoni. He succeeded in carrying it and destroying the outworks by a manifestation of personal bravery, which recalls the prowess of the first Napoleon three centuries and a half later. This happened at the close of December, 1452. In the meantime William of Montferrat, in the pay of King Alfonzo of Naples, who was in alliance with the Venetians, had made a successful attack on the territory of Alessandria, and had reduced many of the castles to subjection. He then moved on towards Tortona and Pavia. Sforza sent Colleoni to oppose his progress; he was joined by Rainald de Dudresnay, whom he had previously taken prisoner at the battle of Bosco. He was that time acting as governor of the city of Asti for the King of France. Sforza now received a new ally in the person of René of Anjou, the titular King of Naples, who had received a large subsidy from the Florentines to take part in the war. He arrived at Alessandria with thirty-five squadrons of picked cavalry, and two thousand foot soldiers. As René was closely connected with the house of Montferrat, he attempted to make peace between the contending hosts. Colleoni suspecting that his object was only to gain time, made a sudden attack on the castle of Borgo San Martino, and succeeded in capturing it. This led to a peace between the Marquis of Montferrat and the Duke of Milan, which was finally concluded on September 15th, 1453.

In the absence of Colleoni things had been going better for the Venetians in the territory of Brescia. They succeeded in taking the fortress of Manerbio, but Gentile di Lionessa was killed in the assault, and was succeeded in the command of the army by Jacopo Piccinino. The new general, whom Spino calls a fierce and warlike youth, got possession of Pontevico, and obtained command of the passage over the Oglio. Colleoni joined Sforza with his combined forces at Ghede. A council of war was held, in which the opinion of Colleoni, first to secure the country between the Oglio and the Adda, prevailed over that of Gonzaga, who proposed to march into the Veronese. With the help of the reinforcements Pontevico was soon recovered, the French troops exhibiting their accustomed cruelty and inhumanity. All the castles in that district except Martinengo and Soncino were recovered. The Venetians evacuated the country, retreating towards Brescia, and Colleoni hastened to recover his ancient fiefs by his personal influence. He soon succeeded in reducing Martinengo, Romano, Covo, and Trescorre, under the authority of the Duke. Rovato fell on November 7th, 1453, Orzi on the 22nd of the same month. Then Colleoni turned to the conquest of Palazzuolo and Iseo, and avoiding the lake of Iseo, which was dominated by a Venetian flotilla, he marched into the Val Camonica and took Breno, the capital of the valley, on February 24th, 1454. Sforza now confirmed Colleoni in the free signory of his old possessions, Martinengo and Romano, with the addition of the important fiefs of Urgnano and Cologno, on the other side of the Serio. The Val Camonica was only reduced after repeated efforts. Starting from Clusone Colleoni descended the Val Seriano, which was firm in its allegiance to Venice. At Nembro he defeated Ludovico Malvezzi, and captured the castles of Brivio and Baiedo in the Val Sassina. Bergamo itself remained faithful to Venice, and Colleoni had too much affection for his ancestral city to take it by storm.

Nothing is more remarkable in Colleoni's career than the skill with which he adapted himself to circumstances. Spino tells us that while engaged in the Val Seriana, in the depth of winter, he conceived the idea of sending some of his picked infantry up the side of the mountain, where they converted large stones into huge snowballs, which they rolled down upon the enemy, horses and men enveloped in coats of mail, and threw them into irremediable confusion. He attacked them at the same time in front, in flank, and in rear. The horses, driven wild by the masses of snow thundering down from an unknown source, fell into the river and were drowned. Many of the enemy were killed, and the rest taken prisoners.

Notwithstanding this apparent devotion to the cause of Sforza, Colleoni was evidently preparing for another change of masters. He was quite ready to pass over to the Venetians if he could obtain favourable terms. Indeed, reading between the lines of the adulation of his biographers, we see that he kept his mind steadily fixed on the acquisition of the fiefs with which he had been originally invested, and which he probably preferred to hold under a republic, than under a master who would be a rival. Nor was it to his interest that Bergamo should pass into the power of Sforza. An event had just occurred which produced a profound effect throughout Europe. Constantinople was captured by Mahomet II. on May 29th, 1453. The last Emperor Constantine Palæologus had been massacred with forty thousand Christians. Great numbers of Italian merchants had been deprived of their property and made prisoners. When this news reached the camp of Sforza and Piccinino, they became ashamed of the internecine war that they were waging. The Pope, Nicolas V., called on the princes of Christendom to drop their private quarrels, and to turn their arms against the Turks. We cannot penetrate into the secret diplomacy of those days, and we do not know what influence this crisis had on the mind of Colleoni. We find proofs in the Venetian archives

that as early as October 12th, 1453, the Council of Ten had
offered Colleoni twenty-five golden ducats.   Also in January
of the preceding year they had made arrangements for
restoring him to his ancient fiefs, and for providing him with
a fitting reception in the city of Bergamo.   Spino informs us
that Madonna Tisbe, who remained with her daughters a
prisoner in Venice, did her best to influence the mind of her
husband in a similar direction.   The knowledge of this
approaching defection and of that of Sigismundo Malatesta,
made Sforza more anxious for peace.   The treaty was concluded
at Lodi on April 9th, 1454.   The district of Ghiara d'Adda was
made over to Sforza, but he agreed to restore to Venice all his
conquests in the territories of Bergamo and Brescia.   In the
meantime Madonna Tisbe and her daughters came to Romano,
where they were joined by Colleoni.

The treasury of the Venetian Republic was in a very
exhausted condition, and was unable to fulfil the promises
which had been made to the illustrious general.   They wrote
to Colleoni on November 7th, 1454, guaranteeing the liquida-
tion of their debts.   Colleoni replied on the same day from
Brescia, in a letter written in his own hand, the greater part
of which is printed by Bonomi.   He explains that he is much
out of pocket, and beseeches for regular payment.   The result
of these negotiations was that on March 10th, 1455, he was
created Captain-General of the Republic; and on the St.
John's day following was solemnly presented with the bâton
of command in the old square of Brescia, the same bâton
which had been given in Brescia to Carmagnola in 1431, and
to Gentile di Lionessa in 1452.   He was assigned an annual

stipend of a hundred thousand *zecchini*. During the years which immediately followed, Venice was occupied by the tragedy of the aged Foscari, whose piteous end has been immortalized by the sympathetic pen of Byron. On October 23rd, 1457, the Doge, weighed down with the pressure of eighty-seven years, descended the Giant's Staircase, leaning on his brother's arm, the same staircase on which he had been installed thirty-four years before. He had not lost the love or respect of the common people, but the Council of Ten forbade any discussion of the revolution under the penalty of being haled before the Inquisitors of State. Pasquale Malipiero, procurator of St. Mark was chosen as his successor. When Foscari heard the bell ringing for the election of the new doge, a vein burst in his heart, and he fell dead. This interval of rest was spent by Colleoni in the consolidation and improvement of his possessions. Besides the fiefs previously mentioned he had received that of Calcinata which lies between Malpaga and the Oglio ; Palosco, situated further to the east, at the junction of the Cherio with the Oglio; Mornico, in the same neighbourhood, and Solza, on the Adda, where he was born.

Shortly after the accession of Malipiero to the ducal throne, Colleoni was summoned to Venice to receive his staff of office from the hands of the Doge himself. He was accompanied by a large number of followers, amounting to two hundred *cavalli* with attendants. A thousand barques met him at Malghera. His progress across the lagoon was followed by a throng of boats and gondolas of every kind, and by three huge Bucentaurs towering above the rest. In the first was the Doge and the signory, in the second the senators and other magistrates, in the third the ambassadors accredited to the Republic. Colleoni was received on board the Doge's Bucentaur, and seated by his side. The Grand Canal was crowded with spectators. Disembarking at the *piazzetta* of St. Mark, the Doge and his guest entered the cathedral, and proceeded to the high altar, where all the treasures of the chapter were exposed. Mass was sung and a sermon preached, after which the Doge, taking the staff of office from the altar presented it to Colleoni with these words, " By the authority and desire of the most excellent city of " Venice, of ourselves, the Prince, and of the Senate, thou " shalt be Commander and Captain-General of all our people " and arms on land. Take this military *bâton*, in sign of thy " power, with good auspices and fortune from our hands ; " let the majesty, the fidelity, and the deliberations of this " command be thy care and enterprise, to maintain and defend " with dignity and decorum ; thou shalt come to no definite " battle with the enemy except by our orders, neither pro- " voking nor even when provoked ; we give thee free juris- " diction and authority over each of the soldiers, unless it be a " question of high treason." After these words Colleoni received the *bâton* with reverence and retired to the palace prepared for him, accompanied by the signory and a great part of the Senate. Ten days were spent in festivity. Two solemn tournaments were held, one of which was only open to commanders of at least fifty lances. The prize was a piece of gold brocade worth five hundred ducats. The other was open to everyone, and the prize was a piece of scarlet cloth.

The first prize was won by Antonello dalle Corna, and the second by one of Colleoni's men-at-arms. Colleoni's name was inscribed among the Venetian nobility in the Golden Book. It happened that the first time he attended the Gran Consiglio a meeting was being held and Colleoni drew the golden ball. In virtue of this he proposed Niccolò Malipiero as Podestà of Padua, which was accepted with great applause. When he left the city he was accompanied by two senators. All this happened in the month of June, 1458, and which of us who knows Venice does not wish that he had been there to see the sight? Colleoni held the post of Captain-General till his death in 1475. The rest of his life was passed in comparative peace, but he neglected no opportunity of exertion that presented itself. He did not apparently engage in any act of war until 1467, when he gave his assistance to the Florentine exiles, as will be shown later on. We have, however, some notices about him in the archives of Bergamo. On August 23rd, 1460, he received permission to construct a bridge over the Brembo, and to exact a toll of one *soldo* for passengers on foot, and two for those on horseback. Calcinata, Mornico and Ghisalba were assigned to him in May of the same year, in payment of a debt due to him by the Republic. Ghisalba was rather an important place on the right bank of the Serio, close to the Basella, where Colleoni's daughter Medea was buried. In 1462 the Republic made a new agreement with him to pay him sixty thousand florins in time of peace, and a hundred thousand in time of war; confirming him in possession of the fiefs of Romano, Cologno, and Urgnano. He had at this time in his pay four thousand horse and ten thousand

foot soldiers.   He appears from his letters to have spent the
greater part of his time at Malpaga.   On June 9th, 1465, the
Venetian senate gave him the power of disposing at his
death of all the lands, castles, and towns which he held as
fiefs.   They also added the village of Solza to his possessions,
as we have said above.

We now come to the period of the war of 1467.   Italy
was at this time full of Florentine exiles driven out at various
times by the predominant family of the Medici.   The great-
ness of that house was founded upon the ruin of the Soderini,
the Acciaiuoli, and the Pitti, who preceded them.   The
exiles who had been driven out by Cosimo in 1434 joined
with those who had been expelled by his son Piero in 1466.
Gian Franceso, son of Palla Strozzi, might be considered as
head of the first, Angelo Acciaiuoli as leader of the second.
Finding it impossible to make terms with the Medici, they
betook themselves to Venice, where they held frequent
conferences with the Pregadi and with Bartolomeo Colleoni.
The Medici, hearing of this, denounced the exiles as rebels
and set a price on their heads.   At the same time they
prepared for war, and strengthened their alliance with the
Duke of Milan and the King of Naples.   The Venetians
did not openly espouse the cause of the exiles, but they gave
permission to Colleoni to assist them.   Money was not wanting.   The exiles were rich, and the Republic was ready to
advance funds.   Besides Colleoni they obtained the help
of Alessandro Sforza, lord of Pesaro, and Constanzo, his
son; of Ercole d'Este, brother of Duke Borso; of Pino
degli Ordelaffi, lord of Forlì; of Marco and Lionello de' Pii,

lords of Carpi, of Galeotto Pico, lord of Mirandola, making in all an army of fifteen thousand men. Astorre dei Manfredi, lord of Faenza, had promised to assist the Medici, but after having received their money he was seduced by the large offers of the Venetians. The scene of war was in the Romagna. Colleoni took the castles of Mordano, Bagniara, Bubano and Dovadola. On October 2nd, 1467, he was encamped at Villa Franca in the neighbourhood of Forlì, when ambassadors arrived from the Emperor Frederick III. asking for a safe conduct to enable him to proceed to Rome and to return. This document, drawn up with great modesty, is still preserved in the archives of Bergamo, and a translation of it is printed at the end of Spino's Life. A battle between the two armies took place at Molinella in the territory of Bologna on July 25th, 1467, the feast of St. James. The battle lasted sixteen hours during the whole of a long summer's day. It was indecisive in its results. More than three thousand were killed and wounded. Among the latter was Ercole of Este, who remained lame all his life. Conspicuous in the army of Colleoni were his three sons-in-law, all Martinenghi, Gherando, Gasparre, and Jacopo. The war had at present effected little results except to lay waste the territories of Bologna, Ravenna and Faenza. Both sides began to wish for peace. Gasparre Vimercate, on behalf of the Duke of Milan, and Gherardo Martinengo, on behalf of Colleoni, began to treat at the court of Duke Borso of Ferrara. The affair, however, was only finally concluded by Pope Paul II., who proclaimed a general pacification on the day of the Purification of the Virgin, February 2nd, 1468.

One of the conditions was that Colleoni was to become the general of a holy league against the Turks, for which a yearly contribution of a hundred thousand golden ducats was to be made by the various Italian states. Ferdinand, King of Naples, the Duke of Milan, and the Florentines rejected these conditions, and expressed their opinion that the Pope should rather have punished the adventurer who destroyed their peace than have rewarded him. The Pope was therefore obliged to give up this article, and the peace was definitely concluded on April 25th. The letter of Paul II., given under the "seal of the fisherman," is printed in the appendix to Spino. It is addressed to "our beloved son, "the strenuous man, Bartolomeo de' Coglioni, Captain "General of us and of all Italy against the Turks." Although the appointment came to nothing Colleoni always regarded the having received it as one of the palmary honours of his life.

That Ferdinand of Naples was an enemy to Colleoni was sufficient reason why his rival, René of Anjou, should be his friend. We find, therefore, that he sends letters patent to the great general dated from the castle of Anjou, May 14th, 1467, by which he authorizes him and his legitimate offspring to bear the arms of Anjou, which were the golden lilies of ancient France, *semées* on an azure field, surrounded by a border gules. In this instrument René styles himself by the grace of God, King of Aragon, of Jerusalem, of Sicily, on either side of the straits of Valencia, of the Majorcas, of Sardinia, and of Corsica, Duke of Anjou and Bar, Count of Provence, of Avignon (Folcalquiero), and of Piedmont. Colleoni also received an invitation from the citizens of Siena to assist them against the attacks of Jacopo Piccinino. But while the Venetians were deliberating as to whether they should give him leave the Vienese chose another commander.

A few years afterwards, Louis XI., King of France, engaged in war with the nobles of his kingdom, made Colleoni an offer through Louis Valpergo, his ambassador, to make him captain of all his armies, offering him a salary of fifty thousand crowns. At a later period, by means of Alan, cardinal of Avignon, he offered him the title of Lieutenant and Governor-General with an increased salary of two hundred thousand crowns if he would assist him with a body of a thousand horse. He did not accept the offer out of respect to the Venetians, for Louis XI. had always been their enemy, and a partizan of Sforza. Lastly, Charles the Bold of Burgundy wrote to him from Bruges on January 5th, 1473, giving him the permission which had never been given before to bear the title of Burgundy, and to quarter the arms of Burgundy, which were the lilies of France surrounded by a border gules and argent, impaled with the ancient shield of Burgundy of transverse stripes, alternately blue and white. On January 17th this was followed by an agreement, printed in Spino's Life, by which Colleoni is created his captain and lieutenant-general for three years, with a yearly stipend of a hundred and fifty thousand gold ducats, paid monthly. If Venice should be engaged in war Colleoni is to be allowed to proceed to the assistance of the Republic, otherwise he is to serve the Duke with at least a thousand men-at-arms, and fifteen hundred foot soldiers, armed in accordance with the good custom of Italy. He is

to exhibit them once a year to the Duke in battle array. He
is to have absolute control over all his troops, saving only the
dignity and authority of the Duke. This agreement did not
lead to any practical result; indeed, Colleoni was now an old
man of seventy-two, and died three years later. The fact
that these exceptional honours were offered to Colleoni shows
that he was more tempted by them than by money. He
always bore the titles "of Anjou and Burgundy."

During his residence at Malpaga, besides the works of art
and beneficence, of which we shall speak later on, he was
accustomed to surround himself with men of letters and
ability, amongst whom was Antonio Cornazzano, who wrote
his life. He was not given to the study of books, but he was
fond of intelligent conversation. He is said to have taken
great pleasure in hearing the opinions of astrologers and
philosophers, and discussing points of natural science, although
he was of opinion that the secrets of nature could never be
ascertained with certainty by man, but rested with the supreme
Creator of the universe. He always held his own in these
discussions, and by his clear-sighted judgment threw light on
questions which had puzzled more learned brains. His life
was religious and his works good, according to the standard of
those times. He was simple in the habits of his life, temperate in food and in sleep. Cornazzano tells us that he
often accompanied him on a six miles walk for the sake of
exercise, and that he wearied out younger men. His court
was crowded with pages, whom he brought up in strict
principles of morality. He was especially partial to natives
of Piacenza, for whom he felt a particular sympathy. He

VIRTVTI DELATA
ARMORVM IMPERIA.

always rose with the sun, a circumstance which stood him in good stead in his campaigns. After a simple dinner he would spend half an hour in conversation, recounting, with an excellent memory, the famous exploits of his youth, talking with the simplicity of his native dialect, and yet with a dignity befitting his age. Some of his repartees are reported. When Cecco Simoneta, secretary of Francesco Sforza, came to Romano to persuade Colleoni to return to the service of the Duke, he replied that he would rather be free. Upon which Simoneta said Sforza would observe : " You " are a brave man, but you can easily be conquered by a few " thousand ducats." "You may tell the Duke," answered Colleoni, "that to his shame and reproach he has allowed " himself to be conquered not by a few thousand, but by a " single Ducat (Duchy)." Once when a certain prince expressed wonder that a man of Colleoni's mature years should allow himself to be overcome by the love of women, he answered : "I am much more surprised that so young a man " should be so overcome by hatred of women, that he could " not even suffer his mother to live." Colleoni was a man of remarkable strength and vigour, which he retained till his death. When a young man in the service of Braccio he could outrun the swiftest of his infantry, clad in his coat of mail. His stature was lofty and erect, and his figure well formed, and well proportioned. His complexion was rather dark, but full of life. He had black eyes, bright, penetrating, and terrible. His countenance represented a noble manliness, combined with kindliness and wisdom. The one fault his biographer admits was a weakness for the fair sex, which he excuses by his desire

G

to leave male descendants. His wife, Tisbe Martinengo, bore him only one daughter, Caterina, whom he married to Gasparre Martinengo.

The great event of Colleoni's later years was the visit which Christian I., King of Denmark, Sweden and Norway, paid him in 1474, of which a full account will be given in the explanation of the pictures which accompany this book. He suffered a severe blow in the death of his youngest daughter, Medea, in 1470, to whom he erected an exquisite marble monument in the little church of the Basella, which is now transferred to the Colleoni chapel at Bergamo.

He died on Friday, November 3rd, 1475, in his castle of Malpaga, at the age of seventy-five. The night following his corpse was borne to the city, placed on a richly adorned catafalque before the altar of Santa Maria Maggiore, and exposed for three days to public view, surrounded by burning torches. His funeral took place on the 4th of January following. It is said that the soldiers of his band were kept together for fourteen years after his death by the authority of his name alone.

THE CONNECTION OF COLLEONI WITH ART.

The life of Colleoni which we have narrated is that of an honourable man—the last of the *condottieri*, but also the best, —one who did not seek to make himself a prince or duke, but who sought a comparatively modest patrimony as a reward for his labours, and studied to surround himself with the grateful participants of his beneficence and good fortune. The closer examination of his life will show that he is more intimately connected with the art of his time than we should have imagined upon a casual observation. One of his principal acts of benevolence was the foundation of a *luogo pio*, a charitable institution in Bergamo, which still exists in a flourishing condition, and serves to endear his name to his townspeople. In 1465 he presented a large amount of property to found an institution for giving portions to marriageable girls, "with the " idea of securing public morality by promoting marriages, " which are the basis of the family, the family being the stable " foundation of society." This was confirmed and enlarged by a solemn donation of many mortgages and other property for the purposes of the *Pietà*, as it was called. The institution was to be managed by five persons. Every year the income was to be distributed in giving dowries to damsels who were desirous to marry, and to two who wished to enter convents. There was a strong prohibition against using the money in any other way. To the ladies of the House of Colleoni were to be assigned a dowry of a hundred and fifty imperial pounds ; to those of the ancient and original families of the city, a hundred pounds ; and to those of the territory of Bergamo, forty pounds, supposing that they could not provide sufficient dowry for themselves. If there were not a sufficient number of eligible girls in the territory of Bergamo, the privilege was to be extended to that of Brescia. The donation was confirmed by the Pope and by the Signory of Venice.

The will of Bartolomeo Colleoni, executed on October 27th, 1475, a week before his death, with a codicil dated a few days later, is a most remarkable document. In it he disposes of all his numerous possessions in the territories of Bergamo and Brescia, and in almost every case he imposes as a condition a rent-charge of a certain amount, to be paid yearly to the *Pietà*.   He leaves all his property in the city of Bergamo to the institution, and with this the house in which he used to live in the neighbourhood of Sant' Agata.   This is to be the seat of the institution, and is to be entitled *Domus Pietatis*. It is never to be sold, or let, or mortgaged for any other use. Unfortunately, the *Pietà* has not observed this condition. Some time at the beginning of this century it sold the house, and purchased one of larger size in the lower part of the town.   The original house is, however, still standing, and the visitor will have little difficulty in bringing it back in imagination to its pristine condition.   It is approached from the street through a narrow passage covered with an arbour of vines. The door bears the inscription, *domus pietatis*, and over the door is the window of a small sitting-room.   The ground floor consists of two large rooms, the outer being a reception room, and the inner a dining-room.   They have been covered with coarse wall-papers, the frescoes have been removed and sold, but they have now been restored by the efforts of Signor Bonomi, and can to some extent be deciphered.   In the outer room, which is lighted by two windows looking out into a garden, there is a noble fresco of Colleoni on horseback, a copy of which will be found in the present work.   The dining-room is approached through double doors.   The little passage between them has on one side a small kitchen for warming dishes, and on the other a wine cellar, both useful for the purposes of the apartment.   The dining-room is about thirty-six feet by eighteen, and is vaulted.

The door stands at the south side. On the west side there is a handsome fire-place between two windows. The subject of the pictures is mainly religious. In the centre of the ceiling is God the Father in the act of blessing. In the spring of the arches are the heads of nine apostles in lunettes. In other places are the heads of various members of the Colleoni family—his daughters and his sons-in-law, the Counts Martinengo. The pictures on the walls are, so far as they can be made out, as follows : on the left of the door, as one enters, is the figure of a female with a dog, possibly Madonna Tisbe, Colleoni's wife ; on the right is the Annunciation. Then follow along the east wall the cardinal virtues—Prudence with three heads, Fortitude with a sword and crown, Temperance with a wine-flask, and Justice with the roll of the law. The figures on the north wall should be Faith, Hope, and Charity, the three theological virtues. Charity is first represented with two children ; then, in the centre, the Virgin in Glory, which may represent Faith ; the third picture, which should represent Hope, cannot be made out. Other spaces on the walls are occupied by the various armorial bearings of the Colleoni family, of which it may be well to give here some account. The original shield of the Colleoni family is canting heraldry—party per fess gules and argent three coglioni (or cuori hearts, as they are called), arranged two and one, counterchanged. For this Bartolomeo substituted argent two bends gules issuing from two lion's heads or, sometimes with, sometimes without the coglioni. When Colleoni received from the Dukes of Anjou and Burgundy the privilege of using their arms, he bore them in chief with his own,

the Anjou arms being azure semée of fleurs-de-lis or, and the
Burgundy arms the same, with the addition of the old arms of
Burgundy, or three bendlets azure.   He apparently omitted
the distinguishing borders which ought properly to form part
of these arms.   Besides this he bore in different ways the
cognizance of the different powers whom he had served—the
biscia of the Viscontis, the eagle of the Sforzas, the lion of St.
Mark, and the keys of the Papacy, the mounted St. Ambrose
of the Archbishopric of Milan.   Further he invented a banner
for his special use, of which the following account is given by
Spino.   He says that it was probably made expressly for the
expedition of the Duke of Burgundy, and hung in Spino's
time at the right hand of Colleoni's sepulchre in his chapel at
Bergamo.   "A man armed from head to foot nobly in the
ancient manner, has on his helmet as a crest the figure of a
lion rampant, with his legs raised in front of him.   The armed
man, with both his hands, which are clad in gauntlets, holds
by the back hair, and forcibly draws towards him, a most
beautiful lady's head.   She, surrounded by rays, with wings
full of eyes, rises breast high out of a cloud—if one may call a
cloud what is a bundle of ribbons, indented like leaves, of
different colours, waving round her heart.   The standard
above and below has two suns, one in each corner, which shine
half covered by the same envelope.   The warrior stands on a
flowery meadow, surrounded by thirteen lion-heads, without
tongues, turned towards him.   All the rest of the standard is
covered by rays and flakes of gold, which sparkle from the
shining head of the lady.   Some of the rays pierce that
cloudy envelope."   Spino declines to explain the device, but

says that the general idea was that it represented Colleoni as aiming at the duchy of Milan.

Colleoni also restored the baths of Trescorre. They had been known since the eighth century, but had fallen into disrepair, and the place had been turned into a monastery of Benedictine nuns. Colleoni had the waters carefully examined by the best doctors, recalled them into use, transferred the nuns to San Stefano, repaired the springs, restored the baths, and made them fit for the reception of the sick. In 1469 the Signory of Venice at his request excused the place from taxes on the necessaries of life. Another important part of the beneficent activity of Colleoni was in his work of irrigation, which was the chief source of the prosperity of the Lombard plain. Numerous rivers descend from the Alps to the Po, but they are violent and intermittent, sometimes rushing with a strong current, sometimes almost dry. They would be of little use to agriculture if they were not cut up into watercourses, which run in all directions, and are the pleasantest accompaniment to the traveller's carriage wheels as he drives along the flat roads. The work was begun in earnest after the defeat of the Barbarossa by the Lombard League in 1176. The Naviglio Grande, taken from the Ticino, dates from 1179. The Canale della Muzza, which gives fertility to the plains of Lodi, was made in 1222, and was for some time considered the finest canal in the world. The Roggia Seriola, made by the city of Bergamo, from the Serio, was completed before 1233. After this many similar enterprises succeeded, which need not be recounted in this place. When Colleoni came into possession of Malpaga and the neighbouring districts, he found that the old canal derived from the Serio was insufficient; he therefore improved it and gave it the name of Colleonesca. He then, in 1473, made a new canal of large dimensions, furnished with mills, saw-mills and wine-presses, which, in memory of his newly-won honours, he called Borgogna. Before this he had enlarged the Roggia Montana on the right bank of the Serio, which was in its turn called the Colleonesca. He also had designs for drawing a canal from the Brembo, and another from the Cherio, but he was not able to put his plans into execution.

We now pass to the more direct connection of Colleoni with the art of his time. On the right bank of the Serio just opposite to Malpaga, the battlements of which are visible from the tower of the church, lies the little sanctuary of the Basella, consisting now of a very pretty church and a parsonage house and farm, with a neglected but picturesque garden. The history of the place is interesting. On the night of April 7th, 1356, a heavy hoar frost covered the plains of Bergamo, doing a great deal of harm to the crops. On the following morning Marina, daughter of Pietro Leone, of Borgo di Urgnano, an ill-educated girl of fifteen, went into one of her father's fields which was sown with flax. Seeing that it was entirely destroyed, she burst into tears and lamentations, and cried out, "What is this, oh, Virgin Mary?" After this she passed to another piece of land, not far off, to gather straw, and here there appeared to her a very beautiful lady in a brilliant dress, with a little child holding her hand. When she saw the lady she began to pray. The lady said, "Do not fear; why do you weep and lament?" and Marina

Arundel County London 1591

answered, " Do you not see how much harm and destruction " this frost has done, so that the poor will have to die of " hunger ? " The Virgin comforted Marina, saying that the year would be more than usually abundant. Marina then asked her who she was, and she replied, " You will see me in " the same place within nine days, and then I will explain to " you who I am, with other matters which I now refrain " from telling you." On the ninth day following Marina returned alone to the same place, and the same lady appeared to her in the same dress. She said, " Thou hast done well. " You must promise to keep yourself a virgin." The girl promised. Then she said, " Know that in this place there is " a church dedicated to me which has long been buried under " ground. Tell the men of Urgnano to dig here and they will " find it." Marina said, " They will not believe me." Then the lady placed three stones in order, and said, " Under these " stones they will find the altar, and when the church is " rebuilt tell them to procure a priest who has never yet said " mass, and let him celebrate here his first mass, and every " fortnight let a mass be celebrated for the souls of the dead " who are here buried." A good deal more was said which we need not repeat. The altar and the foundations of the ancient church were found as the Virgin had described. A new church was built and greatly frequented. Fourteen miracles were performed there. The church was visited with great pomp by Barnabò and by Gian Galeazzo Visconti. Barnabò presented to the church a cross with some of the holy thorns. Galeazzo gave a number of valuable offerings and was cured of his gout. He probably built the parsonage, the tower, and some portions of the present church.

Colleoni frequently passed by this sanctuary on his way to Cologno and Urgnano. He enlarged the building, and placed in this convent Dominican fathers from the monastery of San Stefano in Bergamo. After this commencement he continued his favours, and a year before his death procured the separation of the convent from the monastery of San Stefano. He lengthened the church, and placed a rose window in the façade, adorning the church with terra-cotta ornaments. Here also he buried his beloved daughter Medea, who died at a tender age. He confided the execution of her beautiful monument to the famous sculptor and architect Amidei, who was then engaged upon the lectern of Pavia. The tomb was sold by the proprietor in 1842, and removed to the Colleoni chapel at Bergamo, where it still remains. After Colleoni's death the Basella passed to the Martinenghi, who continued their protection to it.

The steam tramway which passes close to Malpaga first reaches Martinengo, and then Romano, both intimately associated with the name of Colleoni. Opposite the western gate of Martinengo, at a little distance in the fields, stands the Franciscan convent, which was only licensed by Pope Sixtus IV. and dedicated to the Incoronata on September 18th, 1475, a short time before Colleoni's death. It was formed out of a refuge for pilgrims which he had begun to build as early as 1470. In the cloister of the Church of the Incoronata, in a room on the ground floor, is a fresco representing Christ upon the Cross, with St. Francis on one side and Colleoni on the other. The great Captain is kneeling with bare head, and holds his well-known red cap in his hand. It is supposed by some to be the best existing portrait of Colleoni, representing him as being advanced in years. A copy of it will be found in the present work. Below is an inscription commemorating the foundation of the monastery by Colleoni, as well as that of Santa Chiara in the town of Martinengo itself, in answer to the pious wishes of Madonna Tisbe. The inscription closes thus, " Obiit autem Nobilis et Ill. supradictus Bartolomæus, 1475, die 3 Novembris et ideo die illo Fratres et moniales annuatim pro anima ejus celebrant officium ne ingratitudinis vitium incurrant." There is also in the fields a country church founded by Colleoni, in order that the labourers might have the opportunity of attending sacred ministrations. In Romano, which may be regarded as the capital of this rural district, Colleoni restored the church, increased the stipend of the priest, and in return received the alternate presentation to the benefice, which remains with his heirs to the present day. He also provided for the maintenance of a chaplain in the church of San Giovanni at Malpaga.

The history of the castle of Malpaga, which contains the frescoes, copies of which are issued with this book by the Arundel Society, is imperfectly known. It came into the possession of the Venetian Republic in the year 1450, but we have no information either as to when it was built, or to whom it previously belonged. It was purchased by Colleoni in the year 1456 for a hundred ducats of gold. He received it in absolute property, free from all taxes and jurisdiction. It was with Romano his favourite place of residence. It is situated a little distance from the high road, about seven miles from Bergamo, on the banks of the Serio. It was enlarged and remodelled by Colleoni, and still retains the form which he gave to it, except that the roof of the court-yard has been seriously curtailed, thus destroying the great fresco attributed to Giorgione, which represented Colleoni receiving the bâton of commander from the Pope. It is one of the most perfect and interesting specimens of the feudal castle of the latter half of the fifteenth century, built not so much for purposes of war as for those of residence and of the chase. The dining room, which contains the well-known frescoes, is on the ground floor, but the whole castle was apparently full of similar decorations, which are now covered by white-wash, while the walls and floors are encumbered with Indian corn, silkworms, and other agricultural lumber. This is particularly noticeable in the bedroom, in which Colleoni made his will, and in which he died. It is a pity that the Conte Roncalli, the present possessor, does not at least clean out the building from these unsightly and ruinous encumbrances. It is quite possible that treasures of mediæval art may be concealed in it. The walls are battlemented, and in that wide plain are conspicuous for a long distance. The little tower is surmounted by a bell which announced the coming guest, and which tolled for Colleoni's death.

We have already mentioned Colleoni's funeral. The order of the procession which accompanied it is still preserved. It opened with a long row of clergy, regular and secular, the Disciplines, the Servi, the Carmini, the Franciscans, the

Austin Friars, the Umiliati, the Celestines, the friars of San Spirito and San Leonardo, the Dominicans, the parish priests, the chapters of the cathedral and that of St. Alessandro, the chaplains of Santa Maria.   These were followed by six trumpeters on horseback, with black pennons over their shoulders ; a hundred horses with housings, the men covered with large mourning cloaks (*capironi*), their targets on their backs, their lances reversed over their shoulders trailing on the ground, a hundred men on foot with mourning cloaks behind the horses.   Then came a man on horseback clad in mourning with the great standard of Colleoni over his shoulder trailing on the ground, then his shield, arms, and helmet.   Next a horse with red housings and Colleoni's device, ridden by a man-at-arms in mourning with the banner of St. Mark.   He was followed by Colleoni's own charger, led by a man in mourning, the horse covered with fine black cloth down to the ground, charged with the device of Colleoni in gold, and by a trophy of the Captain's arms arranged in the ancient manner, with a sword on one side and a staff on the other.   The culminating point of the procession was the effigy of Colleoni himself, stretched upon a bier covered with black cloth down to the ground.   Twelve men were ranged around it carrying torches with armorial bearings, of whom four were captains of squadrons, and the other eight were knights or doctors.   The effigy was preceded and followed by two hundred torches.   The procession was closed by the nearest relatives, with the Bishop, the Rector, and the Proveditori, and by the servants and retainers of the house, according to their several ranks.

The funeral sermon was preached by Guglielmo Paiello, "a most eloquent historian," and was printed in Latin at Vicenza on January 28th, 1476. He made touching allusions to the trailing standards, the sorrowful war-horse, the weeping family, and especially the faithful Don Abbondio, now deserted by his master. Don Abbondio of Como was Colleoni's intendant, and is described by Cornazzano as being the chief depositary of his secrets. The closing days of winter he says will not permit him to be long. He passed lightly over the events of Colleoni's early life, which seem to have been matters of general notoriety, with copious references to Scripture. He describes him in his youth as handsome, strong, and temperate. He attributes to him the chief glory of the capture of Brescia at the age of twenty-six. He compares him to Hannibal in the manner in which he crossed the Alps and launched his galleys on the lake of Garda. " He was by far the first of " warriors either on horse or foot, he was the first to enter " battle, the last to leave it. No general was more completely " trusted by his soldiers." He was the only leader found worthy to conduct the campaign against the Turks. He records his imprisonment at Monza, the invitations addressed to him by numerous kings and potentates, and the strong desire of Charles the Bold of Burgundy to adopt him as master in the art of war. He commemorates his services to art and to religion, in restoring or founding the castles of Malpaga and Romano, the churches of the Basella, of Martinengo, of St. Peter, of Romano, and the Colleoni Chapel at Padua. He then passes to the foundation of the Pietà, " *Jacet ante oculos,*" he proceeds, " Bartholomeus a Coleo :

" jacet Patriæ Pater, Patriæ Splendor, Patriæ Salus, Italiæ
" Pacis auctor et conservator : animus ille imperiosus qui vix
" orbis ambitu capi poterat, brevissimo lectulo clausus est ; silet
" illa lingua, quæ toties armatos phalanges ad dimicandum
" exhortata est, toties victis pepercit, toties pacem inter dis-
" sidentes Principatus composuit, toties frementi prælio paucis
" cum copiis majores hostiles turmas sapientia et magnani-
" mitate superavit ; jacet Bartolomeus ante oculos exanguis
" et concivium aut militum querelas audire non potest." The
oration then passes to long panegyrics of Bergamo replete
with historic lore. After some further allusions to the events
of Colleoni's life and his happy and peaceful death, he ad-
dresses him in person, and enumerates the mourners : Niccolò
Coreggio, his son-in-law, Gerardo Martinengo, Gasparre,
of the same family, and Bernardo Ladrone. Let them
take example by the life and by the death of the great Captain,
who feeling his end approaching confessed his sins and received the Sacrament, then signed his will, keeping an even
mind in the chill and fever of exhausting ague, and at last
called his friends around him, and leaning upon his elbow,
made them a dying speech.

Colleoni, by the codicil of his will, left to the Venetian
Republic a hundred thousand ducats of gold, for the purpose
of conducting the war against the Turks ; he also remitted all
the arrears of pay which they owed him. He further gave
them the ten thousand ducats of gold which were due to himself from the Marquis of Ferrara. In the fourth section of the
codicil Colleoni most devoutly requests the most illustrious
senate of Venice to deign to have made a statue of himself

on a bronze horse, and to place it in the square of St. Mark, in perpetual memory of the testator.   The first care of the Venetian signory was to receive the legacies given to the Republic by nominating three *Provvisori* in Malpaga to ascertain and to send to Venice the money belonging to Colleoni. The Council of Ten determined that the hundred thousand ducats could not be used for any other purpose except the Turkish war, and should be sent to Venice in three batches at three days' interval.   The money found in Colleoni's different palaces far surpassed the amount of the legacies, so that by November 25th, 1475, three weeks after his death, two hundred and sixteen thousand ducats had entered into the coffers of the State.   These were placed in an iron chest, to be kept in a secret and secure place where the treasure of St. Mark was stored.   Of these ducats a hundred and ninety thousand were to be reserved for the war against the Turks, or some other great necessity of State; the other twenty-six thousand were to be kept for the payment of legacies.   This money was despatched in sealed sacks, consigned to the head of the Council of Ten, containing about ten thousand ducats each, in the coins of various mints—Venice, Hungary, Florence, Alfonso of Naples, and others.

Notwithstanding the generous manner in which Colleoni had treated the Republic, and its appropriation of ninety thousand ducats which did not belong to it, and which ought to have gone to the Pietà of Bergamo, the signory behaved badly to him in other ways.   The lands of Romano, Martinengo, Cologno, Calcinata, Ghisalba, Mornico, and Palusco had been assigned to Colleoni, first as fiefs, afterwards as free

and absolute dominions, with power to dispose of them either in his lifetime, or by his last will. This latter power he had made use of. But on the pretence of the exigencies and the security of the State the Republic, by a decree of December, 1475, determined that these fortified territories should return to the dominion of the Pope. His heirs were left only with Cavernago and Malpaga, the canals of irrigation, and those lands which were the private property of Colleoni in the territory of Brescia. This was a manifest injustice, for these domains had been given to Colleoni in payment of money legally due to him, and they ought not to have been confiscated without proper compensation. Venice did, however, show a sense of gratitude by erecting a statue to the great commander, not, indeed, in the square of St. Mark, for no statue was allowed to be erected there, but in the square of San Giovanni e Paolo, close by the Guild-house of St. Mark. The wax model of the horse and the rider was completed by Verrocchio, the master of Leonardo da Vinci, and the casting was done by Leopardi. It bears the inscription: "BARTHOLOMEO COLLEONO, BERGOMENSI, OB MILITARE IMPERIUM OPTIME GESTUM," and is, perhaps, the most enduring monument of his fame.

THE VISIT OF KING CHRISTIAN I. OF DENMARK TO BARTOLOMEO COLLEONI AT MALPAGA.

It only remains for us to give an account of the visit of Christian, King of Denmark, to Colleoni, at Malpaga, which is the immediate subject of the frescoes which accompany this work. Christian I., Duke of Schleswig and Holstein, Count of Oldenburg and Delmenhorst, King of Denmark, Sweden, and Norway, was a remarkable man. He was born in 1426, and was therefore at the time of his visit to Colleoni forty-eight years of age. He died in 1481. He was son of Count Dietrich, of Oldenburg, and Heiling, sister of Adolf VIII., Duke of Schleswig and Count of Holstein. He succeeded to the throne of Denmark in 1448, marrying the widow of the former King Christof. In 1450 he was recognized as King of Norway, which was then indissolubly bound to Denmark. He received the crown of Sweden by the defeat of Karl Knudson in 1457. On the death of his uncle Adolf in 1459, he laid claim to the provinces of Schleswig and Holstein, and in March he concluded the celebrated Handfeste, a compact by which the two provinces were never to be divided, which became of great importance four centuries later. He lost the Swedish crown in 1467, which passed first to Karl Knudson and then to Sten Sture. His daughter, Margaret, married James, King of Scotland, in 1468, and brought with her as a dowry the Orkney and Shetland Islands.

An account of King Christian's famous pilgrimage to Rome in 1474, has been transcribed from a Holstein chronicle by Hvitfeld in his historical account of Christian I., printed at Copenhagen in 1599. The narrative, obviously written by an eye-witness, is so naive and picturesque that it has been thought worth while to give the whole of it in this place.

" In the year 1474, King Christian went to Rome, of his " great piety, pilgrimwise, to visit the church of St. Peter and " St. Paul as was the custom in those days.

" And that it may be known how such journey went off,

" I have here shortly introduced from the Holstein chronicle
" the particulars of the said journey.

" In 1474 on the Sunday next after the Epiphany, which
" was January 8th, King Christian travelled from Segeberg
" to Reinfeld, and from thence Romewards.

" He took with him from his realms and principality
" prelates, knights and their servants, together with 150 horses
" besides the following princes and prelates, his Highness
" Duke John of Saxony and Lauenburg, with sixteen horses,
" the most noble Borckard, Count of Millingen and Barby
" with eight horses ; the most noble Louis, Count of Heiffen-
" steen, with five horses ; three doctors, to wit, Dr. Henry
" Sanckensted, Dr. Herman Reinsberg, and Dr. John Hessen,
" with ten horses. Also two heralds there and back.

" The King and his suite, as well as the other lords and
" prelates had all put on black, and had caused to be embroi-
" dered thereon white pilgrims' staves. Great honour was
" shown to them on the journey by many princes, prelates,
" and towns.

" The King, with the before-named lords and princes,
" arrived on February 8th at Rothenburg on the Tauber, to the
" marches whereof the Emperor Frederick sent to meet them,
" his son Maximilian, with electors and other princes, he,
" the Prince, had with him about five hundred horses, and
" received the King of Denmark with imperial pomp.
" There he remained with the Emperor seven days, and
" spoke with him of divers matters. Among other things the
" King said to the Emperor that there was a people in the
" Roman realms hard by his own domains, called the Dit-

" marchers, who were most noxious to all their neighbours
" round about and would submit to none, and he desired
" the Emperor, of his imperial authority, to give unto him
" this same people inasmuch as it was not good that this
" people should live without court or prince, and he desired
" moreover that his imperial majesty would graciously make
" a duchy of the three lands, Holstein, Stormarch, and
" Ditmarch.

" The Emperor made no difficulty about it, gave him
" Ditmarch in fief, made of the three counties a duchy, and
" invested the King with it as is proved by the golden bull,
" and other duly sealed electoral letters of endowment which
" were given to him.

" On February 24th, King Christian came to Innsbruck,
" whither Duke Sigismund of Austria sent his consort, the
" Scotch king's daughter, to meet him with three gilded
" carriages, filled with dames and damsels, and five dames and
" damsels on horseback.   And he himself came to meet him
" with 300 horses.

" And he let three pair of them run tilts before him on the
" turf before he led him to his inn.

" The Duke showed him great honour, and the King
" stayed with him three days and three nights.

" On March 11th, the King came to Brixia, and there met
" him there the Venetian Governor with much people, both
" on horse and on foot, and they led him into a palace in the
" town with great pomp.

" On March 12th the King came to Malapago in Venetian
" territory, and the Lord of Hoya came out to meet him with

" 500 horses, and led him into his castle. The next day he
" gave the King an escort to the bounds of his domains with
" loud war-cries of ' Hoya, Hoya ! '

" March 13th the King came to Tarvisium, where he
" entered the territory of Duke Galeatzo of Milan, who sent
" to meet him at his boundaries, 500 drengs on foot clad in
" white, each one of whom had a little banner in his hand
" upon a pole, and on one side was painted the King's
" escutcheon, and on the other side the Duke's, they were to
" receive the King with all pomp and loud war-cries. First
" they all cried ' Christiano, Christiano de Dania,' and then
" ' Galeatzo, Galeatzo,' and last of all ' Duca, Duca.' So they
" kept on crying one after the other, till they came to
" the town.

" And the Duke sent to meet him far beyond his borders,
" his brother and his senate, and much people on horse and
" foot. Last of all the Duke himself met him with much
" people, knights, and squires ; the common people came
" running out of Milan, and would see the King while he was
" yet a good five miles off, and stood on both sides of the way
" along which the King rode, so that one saw nothing but
" people, and they all cried out, as has before been said of
" the drengs.

" When he came to the town all the clergy were in proces-
" sion at the gates, with mighty fine chants, and all the bells
" were ringing, and the people of the city stood at their doors
" dressed most gorgeously. All the streets through which the
" King must ride were overhung with the arms of the King
" and the Duke, and were draped above and below, and

" bestrewn with may and sweet herbs. So magnificently
" was the King received by the Duke.

" The Duke gave the King 5,000 ducats and two mules
" with gilded saddles, together with many pieces of gold and
" silken stuffs. And the Duke caused to be borne before him
" the keys of all his castles and towns whithersoever he came,
" and paid all his tavern expenses. And he went with him by
" ship to Pavia, and there he gave the King a necklace with a
" sapphire as good as 1,000 ducats.

" They lay that night at Pavia, and the King dubbed two
" of the Duke's lords knights.

" Thence the Duke made his people convey him by ship
" to the marquisate of Mantua, Vedian, or Vitteliana; but the
" horses went overland.

" All this honour and largesse the Duke displayed to the
" King, to the end that he might on his return journey recon-
" cile him with the Emperor, in whose disfavour he was, which
" thing also happened.

" March 20th the King came to Vedian, thither the Mar-
" quis Louis of Mantua sent his son and his senate with many
" horsemen to meet him, and welcomed him honourably.
" The next day the King rode from Vedian, when the Marquis
" came to the boundary to meet him with his consort Barbara,
" the daughter of Queen Dorothy of Denmark's own sister,
" and with much people, and received him right bravely.
" And he stayed with the Marquis two nights.

" April 3rd the King rode to Aquapendent; thither sent
" Pope Sixtus IV. two cardinals to meet him, who received
" him there, and escorted him to Rome. There the Pope

" sent to meet the King all the cardinals, bishops, and pre-
" lates who were at Rome, besides the senate, the nobility,
" and the common folk, both on horse and foot.

" They brought the King through Rome to the Pope's
" palace, where he received him and his lords honourably, and
" gave his hand to the King, and the princes and prelates who
" were with him, and let them kiss his foot. This took place
" on the Wednesday before Easter, which was the 6th April.

" The King stayed at the Pope's palace, with twenty
" persons and twenty horses, for twenty-one days. And the
" rest of his people remained at the inns in the town.

" When the Pope perceived that the King knew no Latin
" he was much amazed that such a goodly lord had not
" studied.

" On Maundy Thursday the Pope, in honour of his royal
" guest, gave his benediction to all who were personally pre-
" sent, as well as indulgence, remission of all their sins, and
" release from torments and purgatory.

" On Easter Day the Pope with his own hand adminis-
" tered the blessed sacrament to the King and his suite.

" On Monday the Pope placed in the King's hand the
" hallowed and consecrated rose for St. Peter's Monastery,
" and he carried it openly through the city of the Romans to
" the palace of the Cardinal ad vincula Petri, who had begged
" the King to be his guest, and all the cardinals, bishops,
" prelates, and the whole Court followed him on horse and foot.

" The Pope gave the King great gifts—to wit, a beautiful
" girdle, hose, and bonnet of cloth of gold ; a mule with a
" gilded saddle ; a gold stick, as good as 700 ducats, some

" gold crosses, and an agnus dei ; a piece of the wood of the
" holy cross, and manifold relics, indulgences, consecrated
" neckerchiefs, handkerchiefs, and privileges and concessions
" which he had demanded.

" The Pope also held the King free, both within and
" beyond Rome, so far as his territories extended.

" The King brought with him to Rome three sorts of gifts
" from his realm—to wit, dried herring, dried cod, and ermine,
" whereof he beseemingly distributed to the Pope and the
" cardinals.

" Cardinal Francis of Mantua sent to the King three
" mules, each with two golden panniers and its own muleteer.

" Wednesday after Misericordias Domini, which was April
" 27th, the King left Rome again, and the Pope sent two
" cardinals to escort him over the border.

" May 3rd the King came to Florence, where he dubbed
" two Florentines knights.

" May 6th he came to Bononia, where, in the King's
" honour, Mag. Herman Reinsberger in the cathedral in the
" daytime, and Mag. Johan Hessen at the King's inn in the
" evening, at the King's request, were advanced to the degree
" of Doctores, by the four chief doctors in the University there.

" May 9th he rode to Mantua, where he rested six nights.
" The Marquis paid the King great honour.   In particular he
" held a tournament in his presence, which lasted two days,
" whereat many were thrown, and over 100 spears broken.

" The King there knighted two noblemen, and gave the
" Marquis the Order of the Elephant.

" May 23rd he came to Lacus Cumanus, where the Duke

" of Milan made ready ships to convey the King across the
" Lake of Como, which is twelve miles long, and half a mile
" broad.

" The King in particular had a beautiful ship, with a brave
" and lofty tent therein.

" With the King were four singers and other musicians and
" of provisions no lack.

" There were twelve other ships with soldiers therein, as
" also the Duke's major-domo, with song and music and great
" pomp.

" The soldiers escorting the King sailed in front and
" behind as well as on both sides of his ships, and made great
" pastime with their war-cries.

" And from many places along the lake came dames and
" damsels who boarded the King's ship, sang songs in his
" honour, and presented him with wheat bread and wine.

" June 3rd the King came to Augsburg, where were the
" Emperor with the Electors and many other princes, who
" were there for the King's sake and for divers other reasons,
" requesting various things, among whom were many princes
" desiring his counsel and good offices, wherefore also the
" papal legate had come thither, there the King remained
" with them seven and ten days.

" At that time there was a quarrel between Archbishop
" Rupert of Cologne and the Chapter of the same city,
" for which reason the Bishop had sought the protection of
" Duke Charles of Burgundy, who was getting together great
" armaments with the intent of besieging and sacking the
" town of Nus which belonged to the Chapter.

" To prevent this the Emperor and the Electors, with the
" royal and the papal legate, sent a stately legation to Duke
" Charles, and diligently urged him to forbear from his intent
" and let the matter be amicably arranged.

" Henry, Bishop of Munster, and Administrator of Bremen,
" had at that time, in violation of the compact he had made
" with the King before he set out for Rome, attacked his
" brother, Count Gert of Oldenburg. For which cause the
" King complained to the Emperor and the Electors, who
" wrote to the Bishop, that he should recall his troops from
" Oldenburg (failing which he should lose his fief) and abide
" by the compact he had made with the King until he came
" back again.

" The King composed the difference between the Emperor
" and the Duke of Milan, as he had promised.

" July 1st, the King travelled with Margrave Albert from
" Augsburg and came on July 3rd to Quoldsbach, where the
" King remained with the Margrave seventeen nights.   The
" Margrave showed him great honour with tourneys, dancing,
" singing, games and the chase.

" There the King received tidings that Bishop Henry
" of Munster, in obedience to the Emperor's mandate, had
" withdrawn his men from Oldenburg.

" Aug. 28th he came to Brunswick, and found there those
" whom he had sent from Augsburg to the Duke of Burgundy.
" They told him that he had besieged Nus.

" The King also reconciled Duke William's sons, William
" and Frederick, Dukes of Brunswick, with Duke Magnus of
" Mecklenburg, and with the Diocese of Hildesheim, who were

" all friends, but for a long time had had differences with each
" other.   There he lay five nights.

"On St. Bartholomew's Day the King came again to his
" own abbey, Reinfeld, in Vagerland, safe and sound with all
" his suite.

" On this journey, both going and coming, great honour
" had been shown to the King by many princes, lords,
" prelates, and towns.   In many places he had free quarters,
" yet he spent on this journey 2,500 Rhenish Gulden."

It will be seen from this account that the King arrived at
Brescia on March 11th, reached Malpaga on the 12th, and left
it for Milan on the next day.   The German version of the
chronicle says that he was received at Malpaga by the " Lord
" of Koya," and that when he left he was saluted by cries of
" Koya, Koya."   It is difficult to explain this, but as Colleoni
was called Coleo by his contemporaries, the word may have
been a representation of what the shout sounded to uneducated
ears.

The chronicler goes on to say that the " Lord of Hoya "
gave King Christian an escort to the bounds of his dominions.
This would have been probably to Covo and Antegnate which
belonged to Colleoni :—" On March 13th the King came
" to Tarviscium, where he entered territory of Duke Galeatzo
" of Milan."   Tarvisium is properly the ancient name of
Treviso, but the King cannot have gone to Treviso, which was
far out of his way, and which is not near the boundaries
of Milan.   Treviglio must be meant, which was in those times
called Trevì.   Indeed the German version has Trivigli.   After
leaving Milan the King went to Pavia where he took ship on

the river Po as far as "Vedian," now called Viadana in the
territory of Guastalla. He reached Rome on April 6th and
left it on April 27th. He came to Florence on May 3rd,
and to Bologna, having crossed the Apennines on May 6th.
On May 9th he rode to Mantua, rather more, one would think,
than a day's journey, and stayed there six nights. The
Marchioness of Mantua was Christian's sister, not his niece,
and is rightly so called in the German version of the chronicle.
We may presume that he left it on May 17th or 18th, and
reached the lake of Como on May 23rd. This would allow
time for a few days' visit to Malpaga, which is scarcely more
than a days' ride from Lecco, passing Solza on the way. If
this second visit took place it is a pity that no account of it
has been preserved by the chronicler. It will be seen also
that Spino especially mentions that this visit was paid " in
" the summer season " and there would be a great difference
in the climate of Bergamo in the second week of March and
the third week of May.

Spino gives the following account of the visit of King Christian to Malpaga:—"Christian, King of Dacia, returning from his
" pilgrimage to Rome wished to see Colleoni, and to visit him
" at Malpaga before he departed from Italy. Bartolomeo re-
" ceived him there with great and sumptuous preparations,
" and entertained him with banquets, in tournaments, in hunts,
" and other royal sports, that great King marvelling, that in
" an almost solitary spot there should be so much magnificence
" and splendour and a plentiful supply of all the choicest
" things. But what appeared to Christian the most novel and
" most delightful spectacle was the greeting which Barto-

" lomeo gave him.   In order to leave the whole of his castle
" at liberty for the King and his suite, it was very numerous
" (and it was in the summer season), and to present at the
" same time the foreign king a specimen of the arms and mili-
" tary discipline of Italy, he formed at a little distance from
" Malpaga, in a plain by the side of the road by which the
" King travelled, the appearance of a real encampment with
" tents, ditches, and stockades.   When the King approached,
" Bartolomeo came to meet him, mounted on a large courser,
" thoroughly equipped for war, as was Colleoni himself, fully
" armed like a general except his head, two squires following
" him, who carried his helmet and lance, and at a short interval
" his whole band of six hundred horses in battle array with
" his condottieri and captains of squadrons, all in the flower
" of their age, and most nobly armed and mounted, with
" banners flying to the bray of trumpets, as if he was really
" leading them to battle, a sight truly proud and marvellous.
" Christian had amongst his followers a Dacian, a man of re-
" markable and monstrous size.   Few there were who dared,
" none was there who was able to overcome him in wrestling.
" The King took pleasure in exhibiting by him the ferocity
" and robustness of his nation.   One day, when the King and
" Bartolomeo were present, this man had played with and
" conquered several opponents who had come to the unequal
" trial of strength with more courage than judgment.   When
" everyone now declined the conflict, it came to pass that out-
" side the circle, amongst those who were looking at the sport
" was a mountaineer of our country, who on that day brought
" charcoal for the court.   He was a young man five-and-

" twenty years old, with a body very solid and squarely made.
" He observed that although the Dacian had the advantage
" in size and bodily strength, yet he was wanting in mastery
" and dexterity in the sport. Not being able to suffer that a
" barbarian should vaunt himself with so much contempt for
" his own countrymen, he said to himself, ' if he had to do
" ' with me perhaps he would not conquer me.' This was
" heard by someone who reported it to Bartolomeo Colleoni,
" who then called him aside, examined him from head to foot,
" and judged him capable of doing what he promised. He
" had him stripped, cleaned up, and clothed nobly in military
" dress. ' Go with courage,' he said, ' and if you bear yourself
" ' valiantly these clothes shall be yours.' The charcoal
" burner descended into the lists and engaged with the
" Dacian. He parried for some time his extraordinary
" strength with skilful feints, and suddenly seizing a good
" opportunity he curved his head and his back and rushed at
" his adversary. He then seized him under the haunches,
" lifted him up and set him on the ground with his head down
" and his feet in the air to the joyful shouting and applause of
" all the bystanders. They laughed with still greater merri-
" ment when Bartolomeo caused his dirty clothes to be
" returned to the champion, who made a bundle of them, and
" threw them round his neck and went off as if he were carry-
" ing a noble trophy of his victory. Bartolomeo gave to the
" King at his departure one of his suits of armour, a fine
" and precious work, and he gave to all the King's servants
" new garments of red and white which was his livery."

The pictures which accompany this volume give a representation of this memorable visit, and they may be considered as, to a great extent, historically accurate, and certainly as representing the costumes of the time when they were painted.

The first of the series is that which is called " The Arrival of King Christian at Malpaga." We see the drawbridge of the castle much as it exists at the present day; over the doorway are the arms of Colleoni, and beneath them the lions of Denmark. Round the castle are the tents of which Spino speaks. Colleoni, clad in coat of mail, with a rich surcoat charged with his own bearings, wearing a cap on his head instead of a helmet, receives the King of Denmark. Close by are a body of men-at-arms, a troop of Colleoni's, with two banners bearing his well-known devices. It is impossible to identify the various figures, but we may suppose that the horseman with the plumed cap in Colleoni's colours was one of his principal Condottieri, or perhaps a Martinengo, one of his sons-in-law. Behind him a mailed figure riding a prancing steed bears aloft the banner of Denmark, and the figure still further to the left, mounted on a white horse with a fur coat over his suit of mail, and a staff in his hand, may be the Duke of Lauenburg, who was Christian's principal companion on his pilgrimage. The little boy on a white charger to the right of the picture is probably one of Colleoni's grandchildren. The whole scene is full of vigour and animation. It is impossible to say in what order the events connected with King Christian's stay at Malpaga took place. We will, however, next describe the scene of the tournament. The lists are obviously arranged just outside the castle of

Malpaga.   There is a view of Bergamo in the distance easily
recognizable by anyone who knows it in its present condition.
The lists are composed of two narrow gangways parallel to
each other, divided by a strong barrier of planks, so that the
contending knights might reach each other with their spears
without the horses colliding.   The hills in the distance are
still apparently covered with snow.   It is impossible to say
who all the people represented are.   The two knights
charging in the lists both bear the Colleoni badge.   At the
side of the lists is a small tribune for the judges, five in
number; from this tribune, suspended on a pole, hangs a
handsome piece of gold brocade, the customary prize of those
days.   The King of Denmark surveys the scene from a
loggia at the back, Colleoni seated by his side.   The ladies
occupy one half of the tribune, and the men the other.

Another incident is represented by the Hunt, a chromo-
lithograph of which has been published by the Society.   It
takes place on the banks of a river, either the Serio or the
Cherio, or perhaps the Adda, in the neighbourhood of Solza.
The various forms of the chase are represented at the same
time.   A little dog is starting some wild fowl to be pursued by
a hawk, which a mounted attendant holds on his wrist.   In the
sky a hawk is seen striking its prey.   In one part of the
meadow the deer hounds have run down a stag, which men
are preparing to despatch with their spears.   In another part
greyhounds are coursing a hare.   Two squires in Colleoni's
livery hold a greyhound in slip.   King Christian is represented as a noble figure riding on a black horse, he has a
grey beard, and looks older than his forty-eight years.

COPY OF THE LETTER IN COLLEONI'S AUTOGRAPH.

WITH ABBREVIATIONS.

Vicario de Valle de Calepio. Sul comptito novamt facto fate allogiare in quella Valle Fiordo da Castello ñro homo darme. p cavalli quattro, et fatelo allogiare nel locho de Tayu. latri poi cħ manderemo li farete allogiare con più comodita de li' homej et ancho Achonzo de soldati, facendogli p̄vedere de stantia cŏmo, stantie strame legne massaritie et herbe sŏ lordine de la ñ. S.S. et non marcħ. Dal̄ Rumanj die p°. maij 1458.

BARTHOLAMEUS COLIONUS
Capits gñalis.

WITHOUT ABBREVIATIONS.

Vicario de Valle de Calepio. Sul compartito novamente facto fate allogiare in quella valle Fiordo da Castello. nostro homo d'arme per cavalli quattro, et fatelo allogiare nel locho de Tayu (*Tagliuno*). L'altri poi che manderemo li farete allogiare con più comodità de l'altri homeni et ancho Aconzo de soldati, facendogli provedere de stantia comoda, stantie strame legne massaritie et herbe secondo l'hordine de la nostra S.S. et non mancherete. Datum Rumanj die primo Maij 1458.

BARTHOLOMEUS COLIONUS
Capitaneus Generalis.

He justifies the expression used towards him by Pope Sixtus IV., "Pulchra bestia si non careret loquela," referring to his ignorance of the Latin language. Colleoni rides by his side. It may be mentioned that in this picture Colleoni's attendants wear a parti-coloured uniform, one half of the dress being striped with blue and white. This may have reference to the arms of Burgundy, which Colleoni was entitled to assume by special license. The Burgundy colours are, however, blue and gold.

Another interesting scene is the banquet, held in the very room in which these frescoes are now extant. The King sits alone at the head of the table, the other guests being placed with Colleoni himself, below the triangular salt-cellar. By his side stands the grey-bearded seneschal, whose name we know —Alberto dei Quarenghi—with a napkin over his shoulder, carving a bird. Colleoni is represented in profile—a striking likeness. The lady opposite, dressed in the Colleoni colours, is one of his daughters, married to a Martinengo. The dignified figure in the plumed hat is, perhaps, the Duke of Lauenburg. The little boy seated on his mother's knee is one of Colleoni's grandchildren. Behind, three men are blowing shawms, and one a bagpipe; this is probably to announce the arrival of a new course, which is being brought in by liveried servants, preceded by the butler with a staff. The walls are covered with tapestry, in alternate stripes of blue and white. Three bottles of wine in picturesque decanters stand before the King.

Another scene represents the distribution of liveries to the King's attendants, as described by Spino. This took place in the courtyard of the castle, probably on the morning of the King's departure. Colleoni is seated by a table on which the liveries are displayed, and is represented as giving one to a man who is taking off his hat in acknowledgment. At the other end of the picture the liveries are being packed up in readiness for the journey. The King of Denmark is not present. It was a lucky circumstance that Colleoni's own colours were the same as those of Denmark—red and white. A conspicuous figure in the central group is the King's trumpeter. From his trumpet, which is suspended over his shoulders, hangs the blazon of the Danish arms. The floor is composed of red brick, as is customary in Italian houses. Two staircases lead up from the courtyard, and could doubtless be identified at the present day.

The last picture of the series is the Departure of King Christian from Malpaga. A noble company of men-at-arms in full martial equipment rides along the hollow road. The King's trumpeter, with the three lions of Denmark, is a conspicuous object, on a white horse. Behind him two of Colleoni's trumpeters are sounding a fanfare; we know the name of one of them—Lorenzo della Scarperia. King Christian and his host ride side by side. A Dane in fur mantle and cap is crossing the drawbridge, while another company of men-at-arms is waiting to close the procession.

Another picture, representing the wrestling match between the Danish giant and the Bergamasque charcoal burner, decorates the walls of the banqueting hall at Malpaga; but it is so much defaced that it could not be copied.

These pictures, whatever may be their artistic merit, are

extremely interesting, as showing the manners and customs of the time ; and we cannot but feel that an age which could have crowded into so short a space so many scenes replete with life and colour, with dignity and magnificence, must be worthy of our study, and in many respects of our imitation. Romanino, the reputed author of the frescoes, was born ten years after the events which they portray. He must, therefore, have worked from the family records of what occurred, although in his own age the life of chivalry was not altogether dead. It is more probable, however, that they were executed by one of his pupils, and in any case they have been since injudiciously repainted and restored.

THE END.

INDEX.

M